ARCHANGEL:

A Hip-Hop Vision of Love and The Battle of Good Versus Evil!

By

John Burl Smith

All rights reserved.   No portion of this book may be reproduced in any form without written permission from the author. Copy © 2005 by John Burl Smith.

Published by Intuit Publishing 2878 Gresham Road, SE Atlanta, GA 30316-4304 Email: thedish@ga.net

An Intuit Creative Ideas Manifested Company Printed in the United States of America

First Intuit Creative Book Printing, October 2007

This is a work of fiction. Similarities between persons living or dead, are purely coincidental. All names and characters are either invented or used fictitiously. Although some accounts are based on historical facts, the events portrayed in this work are purely imaginary.

Contents

Dedication 1
Acknowledgments 3
The Author's Thought 5
Prelude 9
Chapter I: A Familiar Stranger 14
Chapter II: A Dirty Truth 40
Chapter III: By Way of Sandusky 59
Chapter IV: Thanks for Everything 90
Chapter V: A Clueless Companion 109
Chapter VI: Goodnight Jericho 126
Chapter VII: Thy Brother's Keeper 146
Chapter VIII: T.H.I.N.C 167
Chapter IX: A Necessary Storm 190
Chapter X: The Perfect Storm (Beauty and The Beast) ... 219
Chapter XI: A Deserted Landscape 240
Chapter XII: Life's Call the Awakening Heart to Kill 257

Dedication

I dedicated "ARCHANGEL" to my wife, Dot, and the family we produced together. Beginning with our daughter, Laquitta, we learned the demands of parenting. Our son, Yohannes, tested our commitment to parenting, which made us define relationships that grew out of parenting. I believe Dot gave me Yohannes so I would have a reason to improve on my thoughts of manhood. My first child Trammel was a never-meant-to-be child.

So consequently, love was never part of her conception, and a family was never a consideration. Her mother's parents must have felt the same because when she was with me, they acted like I could be a pedophile. Dot was not just my tutor, mentor, editor, friend, and lover for forty-two years of my life; she was the lifeline tethering me to reality. Although she passed in 2013, she gets the credit for everything good in my life, no matter how long I shall live. She taught me what love is, how to love, and most importantly, to cherish the love I have. Her inspiration provided the storyline for this novel, and I used her character and personality as a model for my heroine!

Acknowledgments

It is impossible to properly acknowledge and thank everyone who valuably contributes to completing any effort or task. *Archangel* is no different. One must always begin by thanking their family (in my case, the Lee/Walkers) from grandparents, who go back beyond the Middle Passage, mother and father, aunts and uncles, sisters and brothers, nieces and nephews, and cousins as far as the eyes can see. Then, there is an extended family that makes the task even more complicated because names are the only means of identification, and by treading those treacherous waters, one will eventually drown in the deluge of worthy individuals who deserve honorable mention but whose names would fill a book by themselves. With that as a disclaimer, I will suffer the slings and arrows unleashed by those worthy souls I will inadvertently overlook. Therefore, in my defense, I will apologize in advance.

Thanks to my readers, character models, mentors,

motivators, supporters, and believers, Dot M. Smith, Yohannes Sharriff Smith, Laquitta D. Perkins, Tre', Ty, Toi, and Tahlia Perkins Christina Reyes, Wayne Perry, Richard L. Kirksey, Robert Dismukes, Ashrita, Otis and Willie M. Gray, Former Congressman Harold E. Ford, Vincent E. Taylor, Rep. Dedrick "Teddy" Withers (TN), Virginia and Elbert C. Haynes, Charles Cabbage, Molly C. Al-Ghani, Roslyn R. Jackson, Dr. Milton Trapold, State Sen. Katherine Bowers (TN), Dr. Martin Luther King, Jr., Rev. Hosea Williams, Rev. C. M. Lee and members of the Pilgrim Rest Baptist Church (Memphis, TN).

As a special thank-you and in memory of "Harlem Renaissance" writer and poet Mrs. Margaret Danner, a part of the proceeds from the sale of this book will be donated in her honor to the **United Negro College Fund (UNCF)**. Mrs. Danner taught me creative writing at LeMoyne-Owen College in Memphis, Tennessee, one of one hundred and seven historically black colleges and universities in the United States of America that deserve everyone's support. She profoundly affected me as a student, writer, and citizen of the world.

The Author's Thought

I'm a lover of mysteries. I believe there is no greater mystery than a love story. Love stories can be wrapped in adventure, swashbuckling action, intense drama, edge-of-your-seat horror, or the mundane existence of an everyday housewife. No matter their cloak, the emotions of a love story can enthrall, trapping the imagination and propelling the mind to places one has never dreamed of going. Archangel is such a boy meets girl story. Although it is fiction, the characters are real, and their struggles are the inner battles we all wage daily as we search for meaning in our own lives. The key to enjoying any love story is to become the story and live it out through the characters as their lives unfold.

Here's the proposition. Since life is filled with contradictions and irony, nothing is truly what it seems on the surface. So, how does one know they are choosing good over evil when life constantly disguises the choices? What to do? This is a major question for all human beings. It arises from the dilemma, Who am I, and why am I here? This proposition begs such questions as, is life preordained, controlled by some inalterable plan? Are humans fated and trapped in destiny without choice, or are we the products of our environment, shaped by external forces? Could it be we are personalities that respond to environmental stimuli from some basic understanding of ourselves to which only the individual has access?

Simply put, without the environmental clues or cultural milieu, which tell us who we are, where we are, how we got here, why we are here, and when all of this began, will one's responses be the same, even though we have no idea who we are or will one draw a new identity through adaption to the new environment based entirely on external clues? This story is about how life provided such choices and the resulting encounters. I hope, by reading Archangel, readers are provoked to ask questions they have never asked about their own lives. Moreover, I hope such questions force readers to look anew at who they are and what they will do with the time they have left. Hopefully, they will embrace the time they have left as an opportunity to grow. My growth process taught me that humans are capable of aspiring and can inspire as well!

Journey

By Yohannes Sharriff

Journey

The seeker's restless soul, Travels down life's long road

The constant search for purpose and meaning gleams bright.

Guided by some undeniable force working from within, One is driven on to some unknown destination.

Each mile a new experience to cherish, Each town a new treasure to be claimed And for the traveler,

It is the voyage on life's uncharted seas That is the reward that fills the treasure chest

Not the destinations blessed.

Prelude

Beneath a pitch-black sky, stars look like pinholes in the heavens. Standing in relief against the darkness surrounding them, huge smoke stacks belched various colors. A giant security fence encloses this gigantic industrial complex. The Compound contains several large buildings, with an equal number of smaller ones. It also has a helicopter and landing deck atop the largest one.

Without lights, a lone vehicle rolls slowly up an access road headed toward the facility. The truck creeps slowly to a stop. Simultaneously, the doors on the driver's and passenger's sides quietly open. Stepping to the ground, the two occupants survey their immediate surroundings as though concerned about detection. Walking cautiously to the truck's rear, they quietly open the rear door. Stealthily, figures clad in black hoods filed out carrying weapons and explosives. Resembling Israeli commandos or US Navy seals, they seem to be equipped for heavy combat.

Crouched down and moving with the precision of special forces, they form two squads and line up along the walls between two buildings. Responding with split-second timing, hand signals direct their movements. Deploying as though operating against a terrorist stronghold or attempting to rescue hostages, they wait.

Cautiously, one squad advanced to the corners of one building. Their silhouettes moved out into an open court surrounded by buildings. The led squad's advance is in standard two-by-two cover formation. Unobtrusively, pairs go up each side of the open area, while two move up the center. Security lights at entrances provide the only illumination in the dimly lit court.

Just beyond halfway across the open courtyard, the lead squad signaled the remaining force forward. Advancing faster than the point, the entire group was near the center of the open area; then all hell broke loose. Without warning, gunfire erupts all around the courtyard. Bullets rain down on the attack force out in the open. Surprised some freeze and are cut down where they stand. Others desperately run for cover while firing wildly in all directions. Agonizing screams only accented maddening screams mingled with gunfire. Snipers fire from rooftops, windows, and doorways, penning the attack force down. Those firing from rooftops and windows resembled shooting fish in a barrel. Trapped like rats in a hole, death seemed inevitable for all.

Suddenly, one of the black-clad attackers began screaming, "Fall back! Fall back! Fall back!" With bullets still raining down, he raised and began tossing explosives toward the buildings while making a break for the opening between the two buildings. The fire and smoke from the explosions created a cover, distracting the shooter momentarily. During the lull, the explosives-throwing intruder reaches the buildings. Calling to his comrades to fall back, and still hunkered down, he tries to provide cover fire. His cover fire draws every gun that could see his position. The shots force him to scurry for cover inside a building.

He threw his body against a door like a battering ram. Crashed through the door, his comrades, after running for their lives, follow his lead. Some gunmen began shooting and throwing explosives as the lead intruder surveyed their situation. He observes his comrades, frantically tossing grenades and shooting. They cause a powerful explosion behind him, which damages the support structure of an overhead crane. It gives way just as a woman appears, running about frantically. Noticing the collapsing overhead crane is headed straight for her, the intruder runs beneath the falling debris to pull the woman out of harm's way. Holding her, he looks into her eyes as she looks into his. He pushes her beneath a heavy metal table and shouts, "What are you trying to do, trying kill yourself? Stay there until this is over!"

Collecting himself, he dashes toward the door. Looking before his exit, he sees people pouring out of the main buildings headed his way. Making his break, just before the men shooting reach the opening between the two buildings, he continues his hasty retreat at a full gallop. They start shooting as they chase after him. The intruder slows and stumbles, while clutching his abdomen. His body leans forward, heading for the ground. But, suddenly, out of nowhere, a man appears and catches his falling body before he hits the pavement. His rescuer hoisted him up onto one shoulder. His rescuer disappears into the darkness.

Chapter I:

A Familiar Stranger

Life's ultimate adventure began for me one bright sunlit morning in late summer. This amazing journey taught me the secret of life, which is why I am sharing this story with you. It may sound strange, even unbelievable at times, but I assure you as there are angels and demons, every word is true.

My adventure began while jogging my usual ten-mile mountain path. I ascended a small mound overlooking a meadow surrounded by beautiful tree-covered hills. As usual, I paused just before the trail began its last, long, arduous grade towards the top and my cabin. I stopped for a moment, while I took a blow, drank some water, and caught the breeze blowing down this tunnel-like part of the trail, overhang by trees. I was leaning forward, with both hands on my knees, and as I raised my head, I saw the strangest sight I have ever encountered in these mountains. A woman searching among some bushes and tall grass off in the distance. I watched intently, expecting to see at least one other person accompanying her. Her stranger's attire truly puzzled me. She looked as though she had just stepped off the cover of a Madison Avenue fashion magazine. Wearing a sheer-looking camisole, a mini-skirt, and platform high heels, I wondered "Who comes on a day hike in the Virginia mountains dressed like a model. Not only was her attire, not the everyday apparel for a day hike or stroll in the woods, but a lone female in the mountains was definitely intriguing. More to the point, for a guy whose existence depended on anonymity, curiosity was not the only reason her presence could not simply be ignored. Self-preservation dictated that any unusual sight deserved more than a momentary glance.

Watching her from across the meadow, about sixty yards away, time slipped by as I entertained possible scenarios to explain her presence. Suspiciously, I surveyed the surrounding area, convinced there had to be someone somewhere in the immediate area who was part of this strange scene. I couldn't allow curiosity to draw me out when my survival depended on not being seen. I thought: There has to be someone lurking somewhere. There's no way Miss Madison Avenue walked in here or just dropped out of the sky simply to fill my day with wonder. But still, no one appeared. Thoughts regarding her odd presence continued bouncing around in my head: Even though she was a woman, she could still represent a grave threat. So, a lone female in these woods was not someone you walk away from unconcerned.

A man who needed to remain ever vigilant and on guard against weird or unexpected conditions, I felt I should help, but I still felt I was being drawn into something I needed to avoid. Either way, her presence became an itch I had to scratch. The oddity of such a strange situation, however, had me anxious. Whether I went or stayed kept me engaged long after I knew I should have disappeared into the bush. Her presence played against the backdrop of weeks passing without seeing anyone other than an occasional hiker or two. Sometimes, there may even be a campsite, but visitors to this area were usually nature lovers, people well prepared to be out of doors, properly attired, and equipped for a woodland experience. However, in her natural habitat, "Miss fashion spread" would have drawn googled-eyed stares strolling down Fifth Avenue.

Alternative scenarios and questions kept popping up in my head. This isn't Central Park in New York City or even a tourist vacation spot, so why was Miss Madison Avenue taking a promenade deep in the Blue Ridge Mountains of Virginia dressed like a model? We're in the Alleghenies, a few miles from the state line with West Virginia. This area is well above 3,200 feet in elevation. Consequently, scantily clad females don't grow on trees.

Sudden changes in weather conditions can be disastrous this time of year. Rain and/or snow can come up at a moment's notice. For the uninitiated and the unprepared, such sudden occurrences can have drastic consequences. There are no more than thirty cabins within a twenty-mile radius, I guess, and are usually accompanied by some locals. Therefore, anyone walking around out here didn't just happen to take a wrong turn or simply decide they wanted to see what was around the next bend in the road.

A man in my situation approaches anyone up here with due caution. Strangers, like Miss Madison Avenue, are avoided if possible. If not, they demand close monitoring to verify their real intention and authenticity, particularly if they are strangely attired. The precarious nature of my present circumstances and the importance of this area to some people make anyone poke around, looking for anything more than an idle spectacle. Even rarer than scantily clad females in the wild, a young black scantily clad female dressed in a yellow camisole, a hot eye-popping mini-skirt, and stiletto heels is like a three-alarm fire. Out here in the middle of nowhere, her attire was a no-no. Plus, this stranger seemed to need help, another red flag to everyone up here trying to stay out of sight.

More than the fact that all of this seemed out of place and no one else appeared to be part of this curious scene gave the whole encounter a flypaper feel. Cognizant that revealing my presence could be dangerous, but on the other hand, someone lost in the wilderness could bring search parties, which definitely would create more attention for this area than I needed. Instead of all that drama, the right information could send her on her way. So, quietly I moved closer to investigate her unusual presence. I scanned the trees, as I approached, hoping to see anyone other than her, which would allow me to continue on my way uninvolved.

As I thought earlier, *That would never happen,* anxious and hesitant, I approached her. Still looking around, hoping to see someone who could rescue me from a fate I truly wanted to avoid, I inched closer. I could hear her talking to herself from about thirty yards away, but I was unable to understand what she was saying. Her searching movements in the tall grass seemed frantic and quite erratic; she traced over the same spot. Absorbed in her search, she didn't notice me move within speaking distance. Thrashing about in the grass, she kept repeating, "I know it's here somewhere. I know it is."

Feeling very much like an intruder approaching her, my curiosity intensified, overriding thoughts of caution. I cleared my throat, expecting an immediate startled reaction, but she kept frantically searching. Clearing my throat once more, this time even louder, I was a little bit astonished when she continued obliviously searching and muttering, "I know it's here somewhere. I know it is."

Initially, I was somewhat annoyed by her single-minded pursuit since I was making an effort to help her to my endangerment. Then I thought: *She may be hearing impaired.* So, gently reaching for her arm, I pulled her around and blurted quite loudly! "What's here?" I expected to startle her for sure. But as before, my loud question didn't distract her from her single-minded pursuit. My tug on her arm turned her and brought us face-to-face momentarily as I straightened her up.

A knot on the left side of the forehead of an otherwise very beautiful face caught my eyes as we faced one another. Her face had very smooth but unblemished skin, and the feel of my hand on her soft but firm arm said she was well cared for. The supple nature of it made me conscious of the roughness of my hands against her tender skin. I wondered: *What could have caused that knot above her eye?* Coming face-to-face, I was immediately drawn to her beautifully big bright, but darkly colored eyes. They had a dazed look about them. They seemed to look beyond me. Gazing into them, somewhere in the back of my mind, a quick, fleeting thought rushed past, which made it seem *I'd been here before.* But how could that be? We'd never met. Leaning back as I held her, she pulled her right arm free to point at the tall blades of grass where she had been searching.

With slightly slurred speech, she said, "I-I-I put it-it t-t-there. Sooo, I-I know It-it's hereee somewhere."

Something wasn't right. I grabbed her other arm again and brought her around gently to face me once more. I repeated my question in a softer tone, "What's there?"

My insistence seemed to distract her from her single-minded pursuit. Holding her in full frontal, her face and eyes reflected confusion. Her eyes danced around in her head as though they weren't attached to anything. She continued trying to look over her right shoulder at the grass. Hesitating before attempting to answer my question, her confusion seemed to grow as her eyes rolled upward and the lids began to flutter. She continued stumbling over her words, "It.... It's here-e-e. I-I-I know somewhere. I-I-I um-m-m-m."

I felt the full weight of her body in my hands as her knees buckled, and she seemed to lose consciousness. Her weight became too great to bear, holding onto only her arms. So, I carefully lowered her to the ground. That sticky feeling, I had earlier was now a reality.

"What the hell!" I instinctively exclaimed. *She fainted! I thought. Can you believe it? Isn't that just like a woman? Caught in an unusual or embarrassing situation, they faint dead away. A little water on her face, and she'll come around in a few minutes.* I thought.

There I was in the middle of nowhere with an

unconscious woman I'd never seen before lying at my feet. Looking around quickly, I hoped to see another person in the vicinity; we were still alone. I shouted, hoping someone was within earshot and would hear me. "Hello!! Is there anyone out there? There is a woman here in trouble! She needs help! She is unconscious! Hey! Is there anyone who can help her? Hello! Hello!" My calls were in vain.

No one answered. Looking down at her sprawled on the ground, I wondered, *who is she? What's she doing out here? Where did she come from? How did she get here, and most of all, why me?* Having only stopped to see if she needed directions, now it seemed I was up to my eyeballs in whatever this was, and I was in it, far deeper than I would ever have imagined, looking down from the top of the ridge. *The Good Samaritan was supposed to be a lesson, not an actual life experience,* I mused.

During her brief moment of consciousness, while we were face-to-face, there seemed to be something familiar about her in some strange unknown way. Peering into her dazed eyes seemed like looking into a familiar pool observing ripples made by throwing stones. As a kid, I was fascinated by watching ripples. Seeing circles flowing out from the center always captured my imagination. Although her eyes appeared forlorn, looking into them was mesmerizing. It was as though they reached out and grabbed me, drawing me down into some deep unknown darkness before I could look away. Now, it was as though they'd trapped me.

I thought: *Why didn't I simply keep jogging? I would be back at the cabin by now without any of this to consider.* After several minutes elapsed and she hadn't regained consciousness, I tried to revive her with a few shakes. "Hey! Lady, wake up! Lady, wake up, please! Who are you? What are you doing out here? Are you alone? How did you get here?" She said nothing.

Continuing to look around, hoping and expecting someone to appear at any moment, I thought: *This had certainly interfered with my desire to remain anonymous.* Shaking her didn't bring her around. After waiting a few more minutes, I sprinkled a few drops of water from my canteen on her face, but that didn't revive her either.

I climbed to the top of a hill to observe the area but didn't see a campsite or smoke from one in the distance. I looked for a backpack or purse but didn't see either. From her attire, I didn't expect there would be. Glancing down as she lay unconscious on the ground, it occurred to me; she might need CPR. I decided to check her vital signs to see if everything was okay. Sizing up her with my eyes, her voluptuous breasts dominated my view, as I thought: *CPR might not be bad at all.* My eyes moved up to her lovely face and her deliciously luscious full and inviting lips made me think: *mouth-to-mouth breathing might bring her around.* But instead, I checked her pulse. Chuckling at my thoughts, as I finished her pulse count, everything seemed fine, and her breathing seemed normal. Again, I thought, *U-u-u-m-m-m, so, tasting her luscious lips while giving her mouth-to-mouth was out,* I snickered to myself.

My humorous thoughts were an effort to relieve the anxiety building inside. I fought the panicky urges bubbling up while I thought: *Her problem could be exhaustion, shock, or both.* Either way, I told myself, *I'm sure she'll come around within an hour, but she may need some additional care with that knot on her head.* This was the last thing I needed, a strange unconscious woman, lost in the wilderness, miles from the nearest cabin or settlement, to complicate my already chaotic life. *What if people are looking for her? What am I going to do with her?* These questions were extremely important but unanswerable. *What to do? What would Jordan do?*

I could hear his voice in my head, ringing like a telephone. *Never pick up strangers, especially pretty ones. You can't trust anyone. The first time you let your guard down, BAM! They got you! Your only protection is to isolate yourself from the world.*

I know. I know. I thought as I fought with myself. *But what am I to do, leave a helpless unconscious woman on the trail exposed to whatever? Even Jordan isn't that heartless. He's the reason I'm here. He saved me and had no idea who I was. I could have been an agent sent in to find out about Archangel. But he was right; the last thing I need is a strange woman around. More importantly, I need to know her identity and why she's alone in the wilderness, looking like she's headed to a party.*

What if she is an agent sent by the government or Unidyn? That would mean they're on to me. Maybe, they even know about this place? But, if they know that, they know I'm alone, so why not just storm the place and take me? No, if this is a plot, there has to be more to it than an innocent-looking black girl lost in the woods. Some pieces are missing from this puzzle, I'm sure.

Looking down at her helpless body, I thought: *What if I just faded into the bushes like I was never here? Nah! What if Doreen had ended up in such an unfortunate spot? Wouldn't I have wanted someone to help her? Yea!* Then, this curious thought was in the back of my mind when I looked into her eyes. *It prompted this unexplained familiarity that tugged at my memory. Seriously, could she have bewitched me? Have I been possessed and no longer have control over my thoughts or actions? What to do?*

Then that unthinkable thought punched its way into consciousness. *What if she doesn't wake up, and I must carry her with me or leave her alone unaided?* Sizing her up as she lay sprawled on the ground, she didn't remind me of anyone in particular. Having looked at that body, I would have remembered that ass, if not the face. Proportionately, she seemed about five feet six or so inches tall. I guessed her weight at approximately one hundred fifty pounds. Well built, she was sufficiently thick in all the right places. Her looks accentuated her pure African features. Also, her long thick braids framed her lovely face with a smooth deep chocolate complexion. I certainly would have remembered her had I ever seen her someplace.

Climbing several hills with better views of the area, I didn't see anyone or a campsite. After calling and looking around, I hoped to find someone connected with her. The lateness of the day told me decision time was at hand. *What to do? That was the question.*

voice inside kept telling me this was no ordinary encounter, so I reexamined my situation, searching for a solution. First, her identity and why she's in these mountains, without protection from the elements. Also, people may be looking for her is a distinct possibility. Then her possible health issues are a most important consideration also. Next, for a man on the run from the law, who has sworn to protect Archangel at all cost, if she's a threat, this could be a life and death matter. If I take her with me and it comes to that, will I be like Killibrew? Then lying there where she is, it may be days before anyone happens by. If she's not dying now, she may be dead by then. There are creatures, insects, and parasites that will see her as lunch, lying there as if she's snoozing. Walking off now and leaving her when it's obvious she needs care, what would that say about me?

The bottom line was: Do I carry her to the cabin or leave her where she lay? If I treat her as if she's Doreen and dismiss the risk she might pose, I will betray my vow to Jordan. Thoughts of Doreen's voice deep inside my head won out. Besides, my feet refused to leave that spot unless she was with me. Maybe she had bewitched me after all? I thought.

Not fully conscious of the challenge facing me, thinking about the task, like a man, anytime women are involved, testosterone takes over. I thought: I'll carry her! So, getting her on her feet, I placed one arm beneath her knees, hoisted her into my arms, and I strolled off to the cabin. However, the firmness of her well-built frame belied the deceptiveness of her bulk. I may have been off on her weight by about twenty pounds. Big bones, I guessed? Carrying her, I thought: She'll regain consciousness, maybe even before I make it to the cabin. Then, she will tell me what I need to know to help her. And she'll be on her way in a few hours without any reason to remember she was ever here. I told myself while I struggled trying to carry her.

We were only about fifty yards down the trail when her weight started to strain my arms, as they began feeling as if they were coming out of their sockets. We were still on the level portion of the trail when I let her down gently to the ground feet first. Even though I was a very healthy twenty-nine-year-old, 6 feet 2 inches, weighing 230 pounds, lugging her in my arms, was it not? These were my thoughts while my arms rested.

Desperate for a better way to transport her I concluded, I'll let her fall across my shoulder like a cotton sack to carry her. But, after lugging her just a short distance up the trail, I realized, as anyone who has ever carried a sack of cotton to the weigh-in scale knows, a hundred pounds start to feel like a ton after about thirty yards. And she had an extra seventy on that. Painfully, ascending the first slope, it became clear I would have to switch shoulders constantly or find another way to transport her. I lowered her to the ground once more.

Similar to the way her bewitching eyes possessed me, the desire to get her to my cabin took over. The difficulty of transporting her seemed to overpower my concern for myself or my responsibility for Archangel. My focus became skewed. It became tangled up with thoughts of my feelings for Doreen and the helpless state of my mother when my father walked out. The thought of Black men being so unreliable would not allow me to leave this helpless woman on the trail possessed me completely. It reinforced thoughts of Killibrew and Jordan rescuing me, and I was even more helpless.

Standing at the base of the first rise just before the trail levels off and rapidly ascends, I thought about the problem. Surveying the task, I realized how loosely I'd used the term trail. I faced an inclining wash hewed out by rainwater rushing downhill in most places. It wasn't a well-defined footpath. My jogging these past seven months created it.

We were in an old-growth forest composed mostly of oak, hemlock, hickory, poplar, and pine trees. Their canopy covered the terrain like a humidity dome. Underbrush is mostly azaleas, rhododendrons, philodendrons, and sassafras bushes that grow quite tall. They can restrict the flow of air. Rounding out this list, an assortment of blackberry, dewberry, fox grape, poison ivy, and sumac vines must be recognized and avoided as the trail meanders up this rocky, stumpy, and ditch-laden course. An overabundance of gnats, mosquitoes, bees, wasps, hornets, and biting flies also inhabited these woods.

This environmental litany is only relevant because of the solution to not leaving her unprotected where she lay. When in the military, if I had a wounded buddy I refused to leave behind, I'd rig a stretcher. Fortunately, in the military, a soldier has lots of equipment to construct a litter, but not so for me on this forced march. My choices were limited to our clothes, and because of her bulk, it took a great deal of ingenuity to make them work. Choices are limited in finding support structures along the trail strong enough to handle her weight bumping and bouncing over the rough terrain, trying to make it up the slope.

I had to be creative, which was not my first choice. After locating two good-sized straight limbs already broken off trees for support, I stripped down to my underwear. My jacket and pants became the sling portion of the litter; LL Beam doesn't make shoddy shit. They were strong enough to stand up to her weight. I used my belt to reinforce the jacket to prevent her weight from popping the zipper. The pants cradled her butt, keeping it from dragging the ground, and my canteen strap held a piece of tree branch across the end of the litter to hold it together and keep her feet from dragging on the ground. Her back rested on the jacket while the sleeves cradled her head just above her neck. All the while I constructed the litter, Miss Madison Avenue lay unconscious and motionless on the ground. She was like a baby in its crib snoozing. So, after checking, her vital signs hadn't worsened. They remained stable, so we were off once more.

The meandering path traversed trenches, which made dragging her on the stretcher slow and arduous. The need to avoid hard bumps dictated a cautious approach. Ignoring the pesky gnats, flies, and mosquitoes was hard enough, but the thorn-laden berry vines cut my legs like razors. Making it up the first slope, I stopped for a breather while giving my aching back and hands a rest. The bark and knots on the rough limbs used for the litter's supports rubbed my hands raw and caused blisters. The blisters hurt like hell! My t-shirt was the remainder of my clothing, except for my shorts. So, exposing even more of my body, I ripped the T-shirt into strips and wrapped my hands to protect them.

Committed to getting my unconscious passenger back to my cabin fully possessed me. For some unknown reason, the struggle drove me like an irresistible force. I told myself I wasn't going to let that trial beat me. Thoughts of failing or quitting fueled my resolve to save this stranger.

An incident from my childhood exploded in my head. A day I hadn't ever recalled, so it was as if I'd forgotten it entirely. But this day, it came back like a surreal flashback. *Growing up on the Eastern Shore, we would go to the harbor and mess around under the old condemned portion of the pier. Signs warned of the danger of playing there, but like most kids, we didn't heed warnings.*

We heard a loud crash and voices screaming one day. Anxious to see what happened, we ran towards the commotion. Arriving at the scene, we pushed through people looking down at the beach. Everyone was standing around talking about the sign that had fallen and trapped a man beneath it. He was in about two feet of water. All we could see was the man's head, feet, and hands bobbing in and out of the water, thrashing about under the huge sign as waves came in and out. Everyone wondered aloud if he would drown before paramedics arrived.

Suddenly, a guy jumped from the pier and ran to where the trapped man lay pinned in the water. He took a deep breath, waited until a wave came in then ducked under the water. After the wave went back out, he replenished his air before the next wave came in. When it did, holding the man's head, he dove back underwater and repeated the process of giving him mouth-to-mouth. All by himself, he kept this routine going for the longest time. No one else went to help. He had become exhausted when emergency services arrived.

We watched paramedics bring stretchers up from the beach; they passed by with both men near where we stood. Looking at the hero as his stretcher passed, I wondered why he did that? Why did he exhaust himself like that for someone he probably was not acquainted? Now I understand. Sometimes people act instinctively without any personal consideration. Once they do, the task becomes a challenge they must see through or die trying. Now, except for my boxers, I was completely naked, trying to rescue a stranger.

Ascending the second slope required a different tact; it didn't have as many deep curves, but the incline was much steeper. Fewer obstacles proved an asset starting, but new hazards provided challenges.

Rain runoff flowed down several paths forming a kind of roadbed one could follow. Crossing trenches and walking through clusters of berry vines were fewer, but there were also drawbacks to following the water path. Stumps of young saplings and small trees no longer growing inside the flow way created other obstacles.

Only up the second slope sixty yards, the litter began to pull harder. Struggling with it while keeping my eyes on the summit for motivation, I didn't look back to see why. Like a jackass, I simply pulled harder, yanking on the litter. The small stump that caught the footrest of the stretcher didn't give way with my extra tug. The pole in my left hand slipped, and the litter tipped over. Turning to see what caused the problem, I watched helplessly as my unconscious passenger rolled off the stretcher and back down the hill. "Shit!!" Astonished, I shouted.

Rushing to catch her tumbling body, a small stump tripped me. Falling head first, I tumbled after her. My momentum carried me over her and down the hill faster than she rolled. I reached the bottom first, which was a good thing. Her body landed on me, stopping her momentum, which would have rolled off the trail and over into a gorge that dropped off into the brush about fifty feet.

Concerned about her comatose state after that

tumble, I checked her vitals to be sure she was still alive. All her signs were still stable. Although it was a harrowing experience, I was thankful for the outcome. The thing was, I couldn't understand why she hadn't awakened or at least made a sound. But, I was more determined than ever to press onward with my unconscious patient firmly attached to the stretcher with vines. I began the ascent once more. This time keeping my eyes on my goal, I was far more mindful of what was underfoot.

Reaching the top of the second slope, my travails— the blisters on my hands, the briar cuts on my legs, and the insect bites on my near-naked ass—pushed me to the point of screaming. But again, I couldn't allow my agony and pain to become conscious realities and weaken my resolve to get her to safety. Completely purged of testosterone, my gray matter began working overtime.

Nearer the cabin and less concerned about leaving her unprotected, I left her tied to the stretcher at the beginning of the last upward slope. I climbed to the top and walked through the woods to the drive. It comes up the mountain from the main road. I jog down the tree lined drive, which resembles a tunnel. The driveway has a small hill and around a bend, which ends in a breathtaking view. The scene opens on a tree-lined drive, which gives way to a beautiful vista with a big lodge or cabin sitting at the back of the clearing. A sprawling lawn extended into the trees on the left side of the driveway. Constructed against a massive rock face cliff that rises above it like a dome, with an even larger blue sky as a backdrop, providing a picture postcard scene that takes your breath away.

I rushed to the tool shed and got a toboggan. Putting it into the back of the truck, I drove back to the top of the slope. The four-wheel drive made getting back into the woods, where she lay, a piece of cake. With the winch, I lowered the toboggan down to where she lay. I went down on the cable. I strapped her onto the toboggan. I climbed up on the truck's winch and winched her up. I put her in the truck, still tied to the toboggan and drove to the lodge. Covered with trail dust, insect bites, cuts, scrapes, and whatever, I was relieved the ordeal had end. The trail had done a number on us. So all I could think about was washing it off. We had survived.

Chapter II:

A Dirty Truth

Getting out of the truck, the stings, bites, and scratches all over me from the trip and tumbling down the hill came alive. I looked over at Miss Madison Avenue, who still snoozed, undisturbed by my struggle to get her here. I'd paid in blood for the entire education, and as Jordan always said after many of his training sessions: *One remembers the lessons for which they pay most dearly.*

When I was a kid in Asbury Park, I had no real idea what it meant to be out in the woods. Going to the park was the closest thing to being in the bush. I thought a tick was like an ant; it just bit you. Jordan would rattle off examples indicating the need for a thorough cleaning. Not knowing how long she was in the forest, Jordan's stern warning and equally serious expression followed all training sessions. He admonished; *Anytime you spend more than a few hours in the bush, if your skin is exposed, lay around on the ground, walk through bushes, and especially if you are out there overnight, be sure to spend time in the steam chamber. Just being in it will help because there are insects and vegetation that can cause irritations, infections, sickness, and disease.*

For instance, I would always be full of creatures like ticks, mites, fleas, and fire ants that can get underneath your clothes and some literary nest there. They can bite and sting and cause

serious problems. They also bite other mammals, birds, reptiles, and amphibians. If bitten by the same insect, anything those creatures had, now you have. There are hornets, black flies, black

widow spiders, and deer flies, which cause illness, and diseases, such as Rocky Mountain spotted fever, Colorado tick fever, ehrlichiosis, bovine anaplasmosis, encephalitis, and meningitis.

Not to mention certain types of vegetation you can

come in contact with beyond poison Ivy. Plants have physical defenses—thorns, spines, and prickles—which can break off in your skin after sticking to you. Foxglove produces beautiful flowers that contain chemicals that can cause nausea, vomiting, diarrhea, jaundice, blurred vision, drooling, seizures, and even death.

I always took heed of Jordan's advice and made his steam chamber my first stop after a prolonged stay in the forest. The problem with my no-name unconscious passenger is I have no idea how long she's been in the bush, let alone what she's come in contact with, whether vegetation or insects. There may already be serious consequences that can follow.

I couldn't wait to get into Jordan's steam chamber to relieve my pain. He constructed it for just such occasions. It had been my salvation following many of his training exercises. It always hits the spot. Jordan believed in realistic training, looking like, and becoming a part of one's surroundings. Many a day, I had to lie still for hours during training, no matter the circumstances. One can imagine lying on an anthill and getting bitten or in poison ivy, not allowed to move or scratch to get through one of his sessions.

Jordan created a special mixture of herbs and minerals, which he added to the water in the steam boiler. The mixture purges the skin of toxins and promotes rapid healing. Wearing that skimpy top and mini-skirt, my unconscious passenger had been like an invitation to dinner. She's lucky that she wasn't eaten alive by mosquitoes. Her body bore the signs of their attempt. The steam chamber was just what the doctor ordered for us. She needed to be checked very closely after that tumble down the hill. Possibly, she was out there for several days, which means parasites could be hiding or embedded themselves in places only very close scrutiny can detect. I was itching, so the sound from the boiler firing up made my body feel better even before we entered the steam room. Untying Miss Madison Avenue from the toboggan, it was obvious insects had made a meal of her.

I added Jordan's special soluble oil-based cream to the container of warm soapy water. This mixture helps to emulsify debris because the skin absorbs it. I was very careful while washing her.

After dragging her through the bushes and the roll down the hill, debris may have collected in very private places. Besides, ticks will lodge anywhere, especially in hairy areas. While steam filled the chamber, I undressed her. I took off my shorts and placed my shoes outside. Concerned she had not moved, remaining motionless and not making any sounds, I checked her vital signs they were stable.

Concerned about the need for cleanliness, I ceremoniously laid her on the steam room table. Taking off her shoes, I placed them next to mine. Removing her top and bra, the sight of her grapefruit-size breasts drew my eyes to them. Shimmering, they reminded me of gelatin. The nipples rose above them, like peaks on summits. I thought: *I would love to clutch those luscious sucklers in my mouth.* I chuckled at my thought. Removing her skirt and panties, revealing an exquisitely shaped frame, like a work of art. Her smooth rounded shoulders tapered off into a small waist and flat stomach, supported by well-proportioned legs. Even in the steam room's dim light, it was easy to see she had a beautiful body that was well cared for.

Although still unconscious, I washed her as though caring for the "sable Venus, Goddess of love and beauty". Like a eunuch caring for a goddess, I tried to give her body the exquisite care it deserved. It bore no signs of abuse or blemishes other than the bumps and scratches that dotted the ebony sheen on her dainty skin. My hands glided across its silk-like smoothness as I rubbed gently. My hands followed every curve, trying to locate anything embedded there. Finding the points of a few thorns, spines, and prickles, I removed them. Washing her face, I checked her ears and thick, soft braids for parasites. I found several ticks and smashed them. I sponged off her firm but delicate arms, washing down to her long slender fingers. She wore no rings or other jewelry. *Odd*, I thought, for a city girl.

I washed her breasts, rubbing gently across them. I could feel the firmness of her grape-like nipples through the soft sponge. Wiping over her smooth flat stomach, I squeezed the water into her navel to flush out debris and some small crawling creature. I poked around the area with my finger. Nothing was hiding there. Parting her long slender legs, I placed one on each shoulder. Washing each leg and thigh down to her hip, I flushed the inside area with warm water. I comb through every inch of that area, feeling for parasites and debris. With one hand, I followed the water down into her heavenliness. Gently, I pressed back the lips with the fingers of one hand while a finger of the other touched her warm insides. Touching these places only an invite would allow in good conscience, I recoiled. But, if debris is embedded and not removed, irritation and/or infection may result. Foreign objects could have serious consequences.

Finishing her front, I rolled her over and repeated the washing routine on her back. Removing the tips of several thorns or splinters, my hand slowed over such places, giving them prolonged attention. I traced over the contours of her shoulders, then down to the sloping curve of her rounded buttocks. I washed each shimmering cheek of her butt. Sensuous images rose in my head. Touching this unknown woman, I remembered Doreen.

Parting the soft cheeks of her derrière, I spread her

legs. Pouring warm water down the split, I traced the warned water and felt grit too small to see washing away. Rolling her over on her back, I prepared to oil her down in Jordan's special cream. But when her legs parted, my eyes were drawn to one place. That sight consumed me, and I felt I was losing the war of conscience raging within me. Unexpectedly, when I went for my jog, none of these thoughts and emotions that now seized me. Acting out of concern for her safety, now images have come alive in my head, stirring emotions for the first time that had lay dormant for years. Igniting urges I believed were long dead, this unknown stranger has rekindled and as logs placed in the ashes of a dying fire my emotions and desire have come alive.

Now the heat of her presence is melting away the frost of winter's longing. Such urges now kindled sparks that lay dormant like the energy of a log in ashes, my lustful longings, pain and loss smother and may become a wildfire.

This unforeseen encounter with this unknown and unconscious stranger has caused my burning desire to flame anew. Questions of conscience battled my thoughts of desire for control of my actions. *Does she need such care under these circumstances?* The sight of her sprawled spread eagle on the table drew my mind back to times when I had the true pleasure of a woman. The passions of those times made me feel such longing. My heart pounded as though in the heat of battle.

But if I did more, applying oil though needed, would I become like a sneaky thief, surrendering to the temptation, taking advantage of someone so helpless and open to the violations? Suddenly I thought: *How would I explain if she awoke? What would her reaction to being brought here and undressed in this dark and deserted place be? She would question my motives, if I was motivated by cleanliness or ungodliness. Was I being driven by some perverse desire? Could it be I'm simply fondling a helpless woman because it's been so long since I've had the opportunity to touch a woman so intimately?* I thought*: How would I feel* *if she was Doreen and another was providing care? Would I understand her need for such cleanliness?*

Overcome by fear of her reaction and my weakness, I reached outside the door and grabbed a blanket. Wrapping her in it quickly, I gathered her up in my arms hastily, and dashed up the walk to the front door of the cabin. I thought as I entered: *What to do with her?* I hesitated.

Convinced she would wake up momenterily, I had to decide where to bed her down. But where was the question? Considering my bed in the loft, although very comfortable, waking in my bed, she may come to the wrong conclusion. I decided on the spare bed just off the kitchen. Though kind of open, the spare bed beside the stairs doesn't provide much privacy, but she wouldn't seem secluded. The openness would eliminate the appearance of being isolated. She can see outside and have access to the bathroom. The guilty thoughts that rushed through my head in the steam room had me frantic, trying to compose the best scenario for when she awoke.

Laying her on the bed, I ran upstairs and slipped on some pants and a sweater. She could awake any moment, so I rushed to get her into something before she regained consciousness. I grabbed the first T-shirt I saw. Running back downstairs, I removed the blanket covering her. The deep chocolate tone of her radiantly smooth skin, almost glistening in the reflection from the light in the kitchen, froze me in a gaze once more. Its soft-touch had me fumbling, slipping her into the T-shirt.

My eyes locked on her voluptuous body so easily. They peruse her full frame while slipping her into Jordan's rather large T-shirt, covering her almost halfway down her thighs. Once in bed, I let out a deep sigh! Relieved, I was thankful she had not awakened and that God had given me the strength to restrain my passion and resist thoughts after my passion came to life.

Increasingly concerned about her comatose-like state, I quickly prepared a cold compress for the knot on her forehead and tried to secure it with a towel. I checked her vitals once more. Everything seemed fine. Thoughts of carrying her to the hospital did occur, but that meant filing a police report. For a man who barely escaped the setup that brought him here and now hiding out from the law, proper medical care at this point was too risky, I surmised. Even if no one recognized me, explaining how she came to be unconscious and where it happened would bring me more attention and problems than I needed. As long as her vital signs were normal, she can remain here and I will cared for until she awakes.

She lay in the same bed as I when Jordan first brought me here months ago to convalesce. Now caring for her, I realized Jordan's cabin design was a great asset. No matter where you are, if someone calls, you will hear.

The first floor is virtually one big room. Only the staircase, facing the front door and a half wall that separates the kitchen, interrupted it. Upstairs is a large open bay loft bedroom with a huge closet and a sitting area. Down on the main floor to the left of the stairs, there is a fireplace. Occupying the corner is a computer workstation. A large polar bear rug covers the hardwood floor between the sofa and the fireplace. The sofa is flanked by two sitting chairs, with an entertainment center in the front corner of the room. The entertainment center not only housed a television, DVD player, video game machine, and VCR, Jordan displayed an old eight-track player with tapes just for show.

My favorite room, the kitchen, is where most of the living happens. It fills most of the right side of the cabin. A four feet high partition separates the kitchen from the rest of the downstairs. There's a stove on the front wall, storage cabinets, a large window, a sink, and a counter on the South wall. A pantry, table, two chairs, and refrigerator completes its furnishings.

A breakfast bar with stools on both sides formed the other side of the entrance to the kitchen. The bar extends to meet a full wall at a right angle. A wall forms one side of the hallway extending to the laundry room and bathroom on the opposite wall.

The bed in which Miss Madison Avenue rested sat against the staircase. It and the breakfast bar from the hallway, which ends at the bathroom. A bookcase with statuettes, vases, pictures, and books faces the door and obscures a view of the bed as you enter the cabin. The bed has a canopy with draperies on the breakfast bar side of the hallway, which can be closed for privacy.

The staircase has an open passageway beneath, which provides access to the bath and laundry rooms along the East wall. There is also a built-in closet beneath the staircase. Across from the closet under the staircase is a desk built into the East wall. Consequently, as I said, wherever one is sitting or working, they can hear someone speaking.

I returned to the steam chamber, gathered our clothes, and brought them inside. Hoping she would be awake when I returned, I looked in on her; there was no change, except the cold compress had slipped off. After readjusting it, I took our clothes to the laundry room and placed them in the washer; but before I started the cycle, I heard what sounded like a groan.

Excited about what may be the first sound she made since passing out on the trail, I rushed to her bed. Hoping to find her awake, maybe even talking, but disappointingly she was only tossing and turning a bit.

She was mumbling something inaudible but hadn't regained consciousness. The cold compress needed adjusting again. Relieved she was making sounds and moving, I hoped this meant she wouldn't need a doctor after all. I returned to the laundry room and pushed the permanent press cycle to start the machine. *Good nutrition can aid her recovery,* I thought. *I'll make soup and herb bread while doing the wash.* She occupied my thoughts as my mind mirrored slicing and dicing vegetables for my soup. *What kind of girl is she?* The old Oscar Brown, Jr. tune *"The Snake"* came to mind as a major possibility. *She's probably a spy, and I am nursing her back to health. Does she have a man? I wondered. More importantly, is she married? If she's married, how would her husband react if he knew I'd taken such liberties with his wife? As attractive as she is, why wouldn't she be married? Guys, don't let one as hot as she remains free for long. What could have brought her way out here? Where was her transportation? Surely, some guy didn't bring her out here hoping to make out and abandoned her because she wouldn't put out?*

Consumed by questions while preparing our meal, Sherlock Holmes' old maxim came through clearly. *When you eliminate all the impossible alternative explanations, however unlikely, whatever remains is the answer.* In this case, the undeniable possibility is that this beautiful stranger is an agent for the government or Unidyn, which made her an obvious threat to me, and *Archangel*.

Thinking back over the day's events, how could she stay out like that for so long? She had been like that for hours since we were back on the trail.

She can fake unconsciousness, you know. I fought to keep Jordan out of my head.

Not even the roll down the hill drew a sound from her. The time we spent in the steam room with all my washing and rubbing didn't arouse her.

Maybe, she took some type of knockout drug or had behavior modification. Jordan continued forcing his way into my thoughts. *If she's an agent, she may have had a clever implant inserted on or in her. They can be very sophisticated, you know? Implants monitor bodily functions and serve particular needs of the body. Their signal can be location beckons.* I felt like I was in one of Jordan's sessions—his voice played like a CD in my head.

She needed to be checked out thoroughly. Rushing back upstairs once more, I got a scanner from Jordan's closet of electrical gadgets. It contained some amazing devices for surveillance and tracking. He had miniature cameras small enough to appear as a mole on the face, yet powerful enough to transmit over several hundred yards. Some devices shot projectiles that sent their cameras or receiver/transmitters a thousand yards.

Jordan had several types and sizes of scanners. I got a small handheld scanner and went back down to her bed. Returning, I turned on the scanner. She was still out. I waved it slowly over her body. It didn't register any kind of impulse. Scanners read electrical impulses or radiation levels; their signals can be intermittent. So, I waved it over her several more times, but it revealed nothing. During the scan for an implant, my eyes scanned the delightful imprint her breast made against the oversized T-shirt. Continuing down to her beautiful thighs sticking out from beneath the shirt, still the scanner registered nothing.

The alarm on the washing machine sounded, so I went to the laundry room, took out the clothes, and put them into the dryer. Returning to the kitchen, I stirred the soup and checked on the bread. She made sounds again, so I went to check. She was still out but tossing and turning while mumbling incoherently. The cold pack had fallen off again. I exchanged it for a fresh one.

The soup and bread was ready, so I turned the stove off and checked on her once more; the cold pack had fallen off and needed replacing. Moving and making sounds were good signs her condition may be improving. I checked on her one final time before I called it a night. Her vitals were stable. Looking down, I visualized her lying on the bench in the steam chamber. That view stirred emotions I could not allow to awaken. Once alive, could they be kept in check?

Musing, I stretched out on the rug in front of the fireplace. I didn't want to go upstairs to my bed. I'd be too far away if she awoke in this strange place. Neither did I want to hang around the kitchen watching her every move like an expectant father. The warm glow of the fire and even more torrid thoughts about her consumed me. Having lugged her over a mile uphill and stayed up until early morning listening for her to awaken was enough to put me under. I lay on the floor as my thoughts drifted back to the ambush at Unidyn and the bullet that pierced my side.

Chapter III:

By Way of Sandusky

Running from the raid on Unidyn, I felt an unbearable pain explode on my left side. A force propelled me forward. My whole body seemed to shut down. My legs turned to lead as my momentum continued forward. I grabbed my side. Looking down at where I placed my hand, I wondered: *Is this all there is to the revolution?* The harsh reality quickly flashed: *The revolution was over before it began.*

I was reconciled to my fate as my body headed toward the ground, and there was nothing I could do to stop it. Suddenly, a jarring force, like claws, clutched my arm and leg, lifting me before my slumping body hit the ground. It was like being swooped up by a giant eagle from *Lord of the Ring.* Those claws swung me over one shoulder, and a voice said, "I got you, Jericho! Hang on,

Kid! I'll get us out of here!"

Coming to rest on his shoulder, I glimpsed the side of my rescuer's face. It was Killibrew, the old guy. He caught me on the fly, lifting me all in one motion—he seemed to have superhuman strength. Far stronger than he looked, he continued running as though my 230 pounds weighed no more than the pack on his back.

Rounding the corner of a building, he turned and fired several shots and back again without breaking stride. My head swung back and forth, draped over his shoulder. Completing his spin move, I saw two bodies lying on the pavement. This chase scene was over for them, but for us, running for our lives had only just begun.

The sound of breaking glass was followed by Killibrew dumping me onto the back seat of a car. He jumped into the driver's seat, and the sound of plastic cracking followed. It was an ignition housing cracking. Seconds later, the engine started after a quick hot-wire. Pulling off slowly at first, Killibrew gave the car gas. The tires spun and screeched as it felt and sounded as if the car rammed something—most likely a fence. I couldn't see what was happening, lying on the back seat of the car. I struggled to lift myself enough to see what was happening, but the wound in my side wouldn't allow it. We bumped and wobbled until the car reached the pavement. Swerving after the car reached smooth pavement, Killibrew slowed, as blaring sirens sped past. It seemed the police were in front and behind us.

"I knew better than to trust that crazy broad. Things just didn't seem right. All those young kids eating up all that shit she ran, somebody should have been looking out for them. This whole thing is starting to feel like something I survived once before. She asked a lot of those kids. Oldmen walk away from this kind of action, even when there's money on the table. I told her: *We needed to take time to check out this area in case things went wrong.*"

"But n-no-o-o! All she said was:" *Nothing will go wrong if everybody does his job. That's what you need to think about your job Killibrew, not mine.*

"Yeah, right! Smart-ass! There was always something strange about that fast talking bitch. I just couldn't put my finger on it. Sharcura D was different. Something hid behind those big goggle-like shades, head wraps, and dangling earrings. That's why I came out here on my own and looked around. If you live underground, you are like rodents and need more than one escape route. I've been in this game too long to trust anyone to protect my ass. Where's that road? It's around here somewhere, I know. I remember that building over there with that huge ass sign. There it is!"

The car turned off the highway onto what I thought would be a side street, but it felt more like Killibrew was driving on a footpath than on pavement. Reaching a wad of rags across the seat he said: *"Here, take these, press them against the wound. They aren't much, but they're all we have. You need to keep pressure on your wound; pressure will reduce the bleeding. There's nothing I can do about the pain. Does it feel like the bullet passed completely through your body? Feel around your front and see if you can find another hole anywhere."*

I didn't think there was, but I searched for an exit wound anyway. I didn't feel one: "I don't think it came out the front." My shirt and the seat were wet with blood.

Pushing fabric into the wound in my back with my finger, I plugged the hole. That helped, and the bleeding slowed.

Lying down, looking out the window as we sped along. Our getaway exit seemed very narrow because bushes were rubbing against the car. Swerving back and forth several times, it seemed as though Killibrew was trying to locate the path or avoid obstruction, He continued complaining about Sharcura D. I'm not sure whether it was the rocking back and forth or my loss of blood that did me in, but I passed out.

Still lying in the backseat, it was late evening when I opened my eyes. Killibrew wasn't in the car. Struggling, I tried to lift my head enough to see out. My wounded abdomen had bandages. And it was a pretty good job. *Killibrew must have patched me up*, I thought. Groans followed each painful move; gingerly sitting up far enough to rest on my elbows, I looked for Killibrew. And just as I raised high enough to see out of the car, he poked his head in through the front window. "How do you feel? Like hell, I know." He answered his question.

"Thanks for getting me out of there and dressing my

wounds. What do you think? Is it

bad?"

"I've had worst and survived." He said as he got into the car. "I went out looking for

medicine, food, and new wheels while you slept. Here, you need food to help keep up your strength."

He handed me a couple of apples, some oranges, and bananas. Sitting in the front seat, he confessed, "The new wheels aren't all that, but it runs." Pounding on the top of the front seat, he continued, "This one is probably hotter than high noon in the Sahara."

Hanging his arms over the seat, he stirred something in a cup that smelt like coffee. "I can't believe this whole thing. Here we are, stuck out in the middle of nowhere, on the run and with no way of getting in touch with Sharcura D. She's the one who was supposed to have everything worked out," he continued complaining.

So I asked. "Why'd you do it, Killibrew? Why did you help me back there? Why did you care? We don't know each other. You probably would've gotten away much easier had you left me. You wouldn't have any of this to worry you if you were alone." I watched his eyes as he caught mine.

"Yeah, I know. But kid, you showed me something back there. How you stepped up and took charge reminded me of someone I knew long ago. Throwing those explosives created the cover everyone needed to break out of what had begun to feel like a trap. Your move rallied everybody, which probably saved us. Everyone isn't cool under fire."

"Where were Sharcura D and Hannibal?" I asked but didn't expect an answer.

"That's what I mean. You didn't just run off and save yourself; you thought about us. I had to follow you since you were the only one trying to provide leadership."

He let out a rueful laugh. It left me wondering, was he just putting me on? While we talked, the sun slipped ever so slowly behind the trees.

Killibrew glanced at the other car and said, "It's time we get moving. Let me help you change cars."

He lifted me as gently as someone wounded could be. The blood on my shirt and the seat must have dried and fused because my shirt pulled tightly against me and sounded like something being torn apart. I put my right arm around Killibrew's shoulder as he walked me to the other car.

Hurting like hell, I could barely move my legs. Once settled, Killibrew started the car and pulled off. Turning onto a one-lane road and giving it gas, the car responded with a whine.

"I believe we're close to the Maryland/Pennsylvania state line. Our best bet is to head north towards the Poconos. If we make it that far, we'll head west through the Appalachian Mountains, then on to Sandusky, Ohio. I don't think it'll be as hot out that way. We'll get a map when we stop for food and gas."

"Why, Sandusky? What's there?" I asked just to keep the conversation going.

"I had lots of friends out that way at one time. I hope some are still around. Back in the 1970s, trying to survive the national manhunt for black power activists madding, Most cats I knew were on the run from Co-Intel-Pro death hunt We put together this plan to help brothers and sisters dodge the FBI. Most were just on some list. Others were running from an indictment, but some were marked for death by Co-Intel-Pro. They needed to get out of the country, so we decided to take the Underground Railroad, so to speak."

"The Underground Railroad, wasn't that back during slavery?" I asked, thinking he may be pulling my chain. Then, to display my intelligence, I said, "It wasn't a real railroad anyway. You couldn't ride on it." I snickered. Sort of playing along, then asked, "What does that have to do with now? All the people involved with it died a long time ago or moved away."

"I did hear you say you went to college as you talked about yourself?"

"Yes! I read about slavery and all of that stuff, but what does that have to do with getting us out of the jam we're in now? Besides, this is a highway we're riding on." I snickered to myself again.

"What did they teach you in that school? Not much,

it seems. Well, whatever they taught you, they didn't teach you to think."

"What? Are you trying to call me stupid or something?" I challenged him.

"Hold on, Youngblood, don't get all defensive. You see, the Underground Railroad, for us, was about not reinventing the wheel. You do understand reinventing and wheel, don't you? Ha! Ha! Ha! Ha!" He laughed aloud.

"The wheel! You're going back now. Were you around then too? I didn't think you were that old!" I mimicked his facetious laugh.

"Is that right? Well, being educated and all that college boy, you know the Underground Railroad rescued nearly a quarter of a million runaway slaves. You live in the North. For all you know, your ancestors could have rode up on it. They didn't have to come up North running from the boll weevil, you know?

Although its tracks ran up the East Coast to places like New York and into New England and out West through Illinois and Iowa, most of its tracks crisis-crossed Ohio. A lot of runaways were from the Deep South, so they had a long way to go. For them, the Ohio River was the closest point to cross into a free state. Also, Ohio's coastline along Lake Erie provides the nearest point to the Canadian border.

Having been so successful in getting slaves to freedom in Canada, we simply identified the routes that we could find and rebuilt them by putting people all along their old tracks. Have you ever heard the expression, *"By way of Sandusky?"*

"No," I responded disinterestedly because he sounded as if he thought he was educating me."

"You sure you went to college?" Killibrew asked incredulously. "For your information, college boy Sandusky was the key to the whole thing for a lot of escaping slaves. More runaway slaves passed through Sandusky than all the other ports like Detroit, Niagara Falls, or New England combined. Located on Lake Erie, Sandusky was a center of commerce. Several rail lines connected there and being so close to Canada, Sandusky's docks stayed busy—perfect cover for transporting runaway slaves."

Turning off the highway onto a side road, Killibrew said, "I'm about to burst. I got to take a leak." After about a mile, he said, "I don't like stopping at busy places unless I have to get gas or something is wrong with the car. You can never tell what kind of weird or unexpected situation can develop. I'll help you get out of the car after I finish, but you'll have to hold it yourself." He snorted a few times, laughing at his sick joke!

Finished, Killibrew helped me back into the car. He got in, started the engine, and pulled off, headed back to the highway. "I don't know about you, Killibrew. I wouldn't have been a slave. I would have been a runaway. They wouldn't have made me work like that. I would have been smart, and I would have figured out something. They would have had to kill me."

"Is that right? Do you think getting captured and surviving slavery was something our ancestors didn't try to avoid or resist? To understand what Sandusky meant to runaway slaves, one has to remember the horrors of slavery. Can you reach my pack and get that CD? Pass it to me."

"Yea, alright. Here!" I said, trying not to groan as I handed it to him.

"Listen to this. It's a spoken word joint. Being a hip-hopper may help you understand what I'm talking about. There were some real conscious brothers and sisters back in the 1990s. They laid down some powerful knowledge if that was what you were interested in. Check this out."

A Slave Remembers

(**Swosh**...**Crack!!!**)

I can still hear that fine crisp, crackle of whips splitting thick July air. (**Swoosh**...**Crack!!!**) Hot leather ripping into flesh... Beaten to within an inch of death.

Those tortured screams, the silence of unbearable pain... Hideous beads of salty sweat creeping into wounds... Ropes so tight hands grow purple and numb.

Forced to live a lie, watching friends and family die.

Feeling helpless!!!

Powerless!!!

Running... running... running away... barefoot Through the forest towards freedom

A freedom... I ain't ever known!

You see, I was born a slave!

We could hear dogs in the swamp.

Men and their horses... that terrified look in Jo-Jo eyes as I choked him to death. "I won't go back. We either escape or die trying!"

He was so afraid, but I eased his pain.

I can still feel those greedy hands groping at my ass, spreading my cheeks...

Examining my teeth!

Degraded on the auction block! Sold! (**Swoosh...Crack!!! Swoosh...Crack!!!**)

Lesson 1: Massa's secret sessions with those young slave boys...with me...with my son!

I can still feel his white hands shaking with

excitement...

His penis ripped thru my rectum.

I remember...

My momma taught me how to please Massa, teaching me how to survive hell.

See, I remember the overseer cutting out my momma's tongue!

The sight of beautiful Black women forced to breastfeed li'l pink babies While theirs starved to death during that harsh winter of '43

I can still see those soulless eyes.

Young and old come to celebrate hatred as they gathered around the lynching tree.

That stabbing pain as my li'l brother struggled for breath!

Eyes bulging out of his electrified body dangling...gasping for life!

Noose digging into skin... His neck collapsing

under the weight of his thrashing body!

I remember my life spent in hell!

The devil strapped me down... I begged and screamed.

I remember that blade and them greedy faces.

A sweaty hand holding my penis... That quick stroke slicing!

I remember working like a beast until my back broke 'Cause I didn't want to remember what they stole!

I remember the revolt of '46'. Hot metal ripping thru my chest! The peace of dying a warrior

I remember it all!

Dear God! I remember.

"Jericho, to draw on the strength of being a true descendant of slaves, you must go deep into your mind and picture yourself walking along just outside your village when some people jump you. The next thing you know, you're shackled to other Africans and herded together in pens. Packed into the dark hole of a ship and carried to some godforsaken place far, far away. You have no idea where you are or who has kidnapped you. Even worse, you don't speak their language, and they don't speak yours.

All you know is that you must try to understand what they want you to do, or you will get beaten within an inch of your life if not killed outright. Your whole world disappeared without explanation. Pain is your life. Generations labored and languished in bondage. Under such conditions, what's there to live for? Why not just give up? What keeps a person going under those circumstances? How does one *Endure to Survive?"*

Endure to Survive:

An American Hell!!! "Dear God make me a bird, so I can fly far...far away."

From the field, I saw the Klan...

Hoods, horses, torches moving thru the twilight Dear God, what am I going to do?

Running...running...running toward the back door...

They already in the house!

Dear God, my woman... my children!

"Nigger, where are you?

We heard you been stirring up some trouble around here." Dear God, what am I going to do?

Running thru the backdoor half crazy, I'm tackled by three white sheets.

He...he...he touching my woman!

He putting his filthy hands...

Dear God, help me! My son lying on the floor bloody!

Bleeding black and blue, What am I going to do?

Shaking and shivering, I know she needs me, but I can't think.

This son of a bitch is standing over me with a gun.

Teaching a lesson he brought his son.

Trembling with rage as they made me watch.

Blind rage as they take turns.

I fight...fight...fight!!!! Dear God, help me!!

She is begging me...not to die.

Begging me to stay down...to stay alive!

She screams at me... "Baby, we need you here...alive! You ain't no good to us dead."

I can't breathe. Dear God, help me!

He's on top of her, raping her!

Still trying to fight! A knife is at her neck. She cries out, "This ain't the first time!" Quiet tears stream down her tortured face And, I... I bury my eyes in the floor.

Screams for help in a silent protest, as the pig grunts, she gasps for death... Breath... straining for a breath free of death... free of pain... free of his stench With fists clinched she pleads,

"Please...please...Let my babies leave.

They don't need to see this! "

Sweating and breathing heavily he quickly finishes.

Standing over her, he spits in her face and calls her a whore.

He turns to me and says,

"Nigger, you're a lucky Nigger.

You better thank your merciful Master that this is picking season, Or me n' the boys we would beat you bloody,

But this way you and your bitch can still pick, the fields a'waiten."

"That CD is entertainment, yeah, but it's about how it was for our people. Most didn't endure, so they don't survive." Killibrew said, looking at me through the rearview mirror.

"Where did you get that CD? I never heard that kind of hip hop."

"This brother is out of Atlanta. His name is Yohannes Sharriff. He belonged to a group of young conscious brothers and sisters out of the South. They called themselves the "Atlanta Vibe." They wrote books as well as produced CDs."

"How can I get a CD or a book?" I asked, not sure I would follow up on it.

"The best way is to go online and put in Yohannes' name or the Atlanta Vibe," Killibrew said, still checking me out in the rearview mirror.

Then he said, "Let me get back to what I was telling you because I did have a point to make. From the time of a slave's capture, they witnessed others die along trails, in pens, aboard ships, and on this land where you stand. Now, because of them, you've survived. Why you? He asked? All you have left of your heritage is their thought of freedom. For them, it was a passionate longing, and their taste for freedom never turned to dust in the mouths of some slaves.

So, one day you make your break. Those slaves that ran to get free, on their run, they carried with them a hope that extended back to the first captured soul. The millions that perished run with them. Running inspired those left behind. They gained renewed hope that they, too, may one day drink the sweet water of the Ohio River on freedom's side.

Alone or on the Underground Railroad, life on the run was harsh, rough hewn, and uncompromising. Hiding in woods, trudging through muddy swamps, wet and cold, with little or no food for days—some even had young children and old folks with them. And this is the point of everything I've said, no matter how hard and painful, quitting was never an option!

You said you read about the Underground Railroad, well then you know Harriet Tubman, the greatest conductor of all, carried a pistol and threatened to shoot anyone who turned back."

"Yeah, I read that. She never lost a passenger!"

"So, you see, Sandusky wasn't only a place or destination, it was a symbol of hope – hope was Sandusky's code name. On the Underground Railroad or your own, once a runaway slave reached Sandusky, they knew the next stop was Canada. Reaching Sandusky, they closed a circle that began with the first captive's dream of freedom. It was like arriving at the gates of paradise and waiting for Gabriel to grant passage.

So Youngblood, before you become a cynic or show disinterest, make sure you know the real story. If not, you may show your ignorance by laughing and dissing yourself," Killibrew concluded.

Saying nothing, I had no idea he had picked up on me giving him attitude earlier.

Nearing the Poconos, clouds hung heavily over the mountains, obscuring their peaks. Once in the higher elevations, we ran into a driving rain storm.

Killibrew thought the rain was a good thing. He said, "There's nothing like a good cleansing rain to wash away the bad vibes and devious spirits in the environment. Those who follow feng shui believe evil spirits ride on the wind; rain washes them away. That's why I say rain is a cleansing action. Besides, it keeps all the bullshitters off the road, and state troopers usually hold up at their favorite spot. They don't like doing their tours in wet uniforms."

Even though the defroster was working, Killibrew constantly wiped the windshield, maybe to reduce the glare of headlights reflecting off the rain-slick pavement. Propped up in the back seat, pain from my wound was giving me the blues, but complaining things weren't going to change them. I simply had to grit and bear it.

Fighting the driving rain and wiping the windshield kept Killibrew pretty busy. After his last comments, I felt his rambling conversation was aimed at me rather than to keep himself awake. So I listened.

Thinking back, Clay Killibrew was one of several old guys that hung around Little Haiti. We jokingly called them relics. He never said much, but when he spoke, people listened. With a name like Killibrew, you knew he was a man not to be trifled with. Watching how he dealt with some people, it was obvious death and dying were familiar to him. He showed up, it seems, about the time Parson found me on the steps of the Parish. He stayed close to things happening around there, although he wasn't a drunk or junkie. I don't know whether he joined BLUF before or after I did, but in BLUF, he was the same as around the Parish.

Providing background music for Killibrew's foray into the past, the rain continued non-stop. Trudging down memory lane with him resembled a guided tour through black history. Although he hadn't received credit for his activities and sacrifices, as he talked, I detected real pride in what he did. I listened to what seemed like a sermon about his younger years, and got the impression that our journeys hadn't been all that different.

"Yeah, Jericho, I was just a country boy shackled to

the land by my family's legacy. Trapped in a socioeconomic and political system that broke black people at an early age, the struggle was keeping the faith. Under those conditions, the best you could hope for was that some white person would take a liking to you and teach you something rather than just taking you into their beds. That was what happened to Jenny, the only woman I've ever loved.

History books say slavery ended with the Emancipation Proclamation in 1863. But for black folks, particularly in the South, it has never ended. Slavery in America was made possible by the 3/5 Compromise of Article I Section II in the US Constitution. The Emancipation Proclamation did not end slavery, as most people think. That's because it didn't repeal the 3/5 Compromise in the Constitution. Institutionalized racism maintains it as the underpinning for *White privilege*. Consequently, economic and political slavery continued for black people in the US. A Black economist, Dorothy M. Smith proved that slavery created the chasm of inequality. She found that the wealth gap between blacks and whites is because of the gap in income and employment. This same gap existed when emancipation supposedly freed slaves. This gap remains because of institutionalized racism/white privilege. Did they teach you anything like that in the school you attended?"

"No," reluctantly, I admitted. I wanted to dismiss Killibrew's comments because I hated thoughts of being fooled so completely by history books. But, I knew institutionalized racism and white privilege ran America. White people had to have some way to keep black people down all these years.

"Land and cotton are what it was all about for blacks in the South Jericho. If you had land, you could grow cotton. White folks had the land, so we grew the cotton. Without cotton, there wasn't any hope for a black family struggling to endure to survive. That grip gave white folks the power of life and death and why down South, a white man's word was law, no matter what. He could take a black man's land, woman, and life, and no one did anything about it.

That was Jenny's fate. We planned to get married, but she lived on Mr. Walton's land. His son, Billy Bob, had been after Jenny since she was a little girl. He wanted to keep her as his plaything until he used her up and didn't want her anymore. Just turning fifteen, Jenny was in a hurry to get married. We set a date, and I told Billy Bob to stop messing with her, but a black man can't tell a white man anything that he will do, and that's gospel.

Billy Bob stayed after her, showing up at her family's place, trying to catch her alone. She would run off into the field and hide whenever she saw him coming. We planned to leave the county late one night, but her parents thought they could talk to o'man Walton, and he would make Billy Bob leave her alone since she was getting married. The day her folks went to town to talk with old man Walton, Jenny was at the house alone. She said Billy Bob sneaked up on her. At home alone, he wanted to have his way with her, but she fought him. Jenny said "I'd rather die than give in to a slimy bastard like Billy Bob. So I fought him real hard." Billy Bob beat her up so badly that she died a few days later."

Killibrew paused and swallowed several time before he resumed. The strain in his voice was unmistakable.

"L-L-Loosing-g-g. Uh, u-uh-h-!!! Losing Jenny changed everything for me. I didn't care what happened to me after that. If a man can't protect his woman, he can at least die trying to avenge her. I swore that redneck would pay, and he did. I hid out watching their big fancy-ass shit house for nearly a week before I caught him alone. I knew sooner or later he would have to take a shit, and nobody wants company then. I crawled up to the outhouse, kicked open the door, and slit his throat. I left him sitting on the stool.

Death couldn't come to him as an accidental occurrence or a shot from far off. I wanted him to see my face and know that no matter what his daddy told him or how many women he'd raped and gotten away with it, this time, vengeance and justice had finally caught up with his sorry ass. And, like Jenny, there was nothing he could do about it. I washed his blood off in a nearby creek, then walked down to the trestle and hopped a train headed for Memphis, Tennessee, an hour later." Listening, I thought about Doreen and understood why Jenny had been his only love.

The rain continued pouring as we rolled westward. Killibrew stopped for gas and food. He also picked up some pain pills, and I downed several after I ate. Sipping on a jug of orange juice as we rode, I marveled at Killibrew's rapt gaze while driving. Talking, he made dramatic gestures to emphasize his point. History seemed to flow out of him like rain rolling down the back windshields from the nonstop downpour. Killibrew resumed his history lesson.

"Jericho, it's up to young brothers and sisters like you now. You guys have got to realize that black people's survival is at stake. It's your time to carry the ball, to push the load uphill a little further than where it was before your generation took over. You've got it now whether you want it or not. It's your time to build a model that creates a positive future and gives Black people hope again—a new Sandusky.

Hope is what your generation represents for my generation, like we were for the generation before us. Freedom is a journey, not a destination. It's like the Underground Railroad. Even though you couldn't ride on it, it got thousands out of slavery, which gave hope to all those left behind. Your generation must learn the power of faith; they must endure to survive and to survive, you must believe.

Leaders of your generation must see beyond the evil that surrounds us. Present-day circumstances and appearances are deceptions to beguile the fateful. They must see with their slave ancestors' eyes to guide our people through to the other side."

Chapter IV:

Thanks for Everything

Killibrew racing down the highway through the rain, water hitting against the car, and sounds from its tires splashing through puddles on the pavement all came together in a rhythmic beat in my head. Lyrics from Yohannes' CD were like the back line keeping the beat of black people's lives, as thoughts careened through undisturbed memories that lay like dust in the attic. Disparate thoughts and experiences regarding my existence converged like trains on the same track. However, their collision did not result in any wreckage but was more like a hard kiss between long-lost lovers brought together unexpectedly. Their reunion sealed a breach, merging the two into one. It seemed Yohannes' CD was becoming a rhythm for the song track of my life. The rain and listening to the rap before then had been pretty uneventful, but now I began to see things clearer.

Killibrew pulled into a gas station to make a pit stop for gas, food and something to drink. He'd selected a little town just across the state line in Ohio called Palestine. He said, "We'll stop here for refills on gas and food. It looks peaceful enough, but you never know. Keep your eyes open for anything strange. We can't trust these rednecks no matter how innocently they look." Then he went inside. When he came out the door, I saw a policeman come to the door and peek through the door's glass. I thought *he must have followed Killibrew to the door.* After looking through the glass, he came out and walked down the side of the building into the shadows. The lights of an automobile came on when he opened the door of a car parked in the dark shadow. It was a patrol car that's when I knew he was on duty.. He didn't drive away. After Killibrew got into the car, I asked, "Did you see a policeman while you were inside the gas station?"

"No, Why?" He asked as he started the car.

"One came to the door and peered through the glass. He came out, looked in your direction, and went to a patrol car parked on the side." I pointed in the direction of the darkness alongside the building. "The patrol car is parked there in the shadows."

"He must have come out of the back someplace." Killibrew surmised. "Like, I said, they don't like getting their uniforms wet. This place must be his usual hangout. Had his car been parked out front, I would have passed this one up."

Pulling off slowly, Killibrew turned onto the highway. I looked into the darkness for the patrol car. Its lights came on and turned on to the highway in the direction we traveled. Killibrew stayed below the speed limit, and the patrolman stayed behind us a good distance.

"Hanging back like that, he has something on his mind," Killibrew said, while monitoring the patrol car through the rain flowing down the back windshield in the rearview mirror.

"Staying back as far as he is, he can't see this car's tag number to run its plate and learn it's hot. He's probably radioing for backup. Maybe his buddies are setting up a roadblock ahead of us, and we are headed straight for it.

I don't want any part of that, so I will take that road coming up. Hold on, stay down. There may be shooting."

Killibrew gave the car some gas, and the steering wheel a hard pull to the right. The car jumped and fishtailed, skidding and dancing he pulled hard onto a side road. I reached down and picked up Killibrew's automatic from the floor and checked the clip. It needed replacing. We were flying down this narrow road straddling the centerline, wobbling back and forth, as Killibrew fought to keep the car in the middle of the road. Puddles of rain dotted the roadway, which made driving a real adventure. Killibrew demanded more speed, slamming the gas paddle against the floor, trying to put more distance between us and our pursuer.

Still giving chase, in hot pursuit, the guy was determined to apprehend us. It must have seemed he was chasing a speedboat, especially when Killibrew splashed through big puddles. The patrol car closed on us as we encountered curves and small hills. Not slowing down, the tires cried and screeched in the curves, and the bottom of the car scraped as we flew across hills and down into slopes of the road. Rather than slowing down,

Killibrew slammed his foot against the gas paddle, demanding more speed.

Sitting propped up in the back and bouncing around while holding the automatic, I could see out the back window and the road ahead through the front windshield. A deep curve in the road appeared, but Killibrew didn't slow down. I don't know how, but I knew this chase had reached its climax. Suddenly, Killibrew slammed on the brakes while gunning the engine. He turned the steering wheel hard and fast to the left. He forced the car to skid, spin, and turn one hundred eighty degrees, in a quick doughnut maneuver. Our headlight became a spotlight on the police car. The quick turn-about caught the trooper completely by surprise. The headlights of the police car wobbled from side to side, and we felt a jar as the car sideswiped our car, zooming past. Blinded by our headlights, the trooper couldn't see the deep curve in the road. His car skidded and flip, then rolled off the road into the trees.

Bumped by the police cruiser, our car ended up on the rain-soaked shoulder of the road, stuck in mud up to its axles. Abandoning the vehicle, we took to the woods in full gallop. Slogging through what seemed a swamp for what seemed like an eternity in mud up to our knees, I held onto Killibrew as best I could. Clutching my side, I nearly passed out several times from the pain. Knowing Killibrew was mostly dragging me, I said: *If you didn't have me hanging on to you slowing you down, you could make better time."* I begged him, *"Leave me! Leave me! I'm done for Killibrew. You can move faster and make better time without me hanging on to you. There isn't any reason for both of us to get caught."*

"No, I'm not leaving you. We started together, and we will finish together. Hang on, kid, you're stronger than you know. I'm not going to let you quit. All you have to do is keep putting one foot in front of the other. No matter how long it takes, the idea is to just keep moving."

Killibrew grabbed my arm and put it around his shoulder; clutching my belt with one hand, he dragged me. Then, the image of runaway slaves flashed in my mind as Killibrew's description of their struggle trying to make it to freedom on the Underground Railroad exploded in my head. Their desperate struggle became a reality as images careened down through unexamined places in my head. Mentally transported back to the time of slaves' desperate flight, I thought, *What would I have done had I really been a slave and this was my desperate flight to freedom? Would I have endured, or would I have quit?*

Killibrew's description of terrified runaway slaves besieged by vicious dogs seemed to come alive like a video. Trying to elude bloodthirsty carnivores, which were raised eating human flush and lading up their blood, once they are on the trail of a slave, death awaited. Growling and snorting, they ran older people down first, next any children that could not keep up. Knowing they have a scent, fear made it everyone for themselves. Nothing stopped their growling pursuit of running slaves down, but a bullet. All these images seemed to materialize before my eyes as though such dogs were on our trail.

Such grizzle images began to spur me. Struggling strength seemed to come from somewhere outside of me. Maybe, Killibrew's resolve had transferred to me. The pain from my wound faded as we clawed at the mud, sometimes crawling to keep moving. Other times, we simply stretched out and slid along on our bellies, pulling at grass and small trees to keep moving. Suddenly, without warning, Killibrew stopped. He took the pistols from his backpack, gave me one, and checked the other for ammo. He set me up, leaned me against a tree, and put a finger to his lips, signaling quiet. He walked ahead. I tried to follow, but he signaled me to stay put, so I did.

The rain continued pouring, washing the mud from my face, so I caught some in my mouth. I'd forgotten about my thirst. After a while, Killibrew returned. *"There's a campsite up ahead. They have a truck. It's hitched to one of those pop-up campers with a tent attached. It seems everyone's asleep. Even though the rain will cover most sounds we make, we need to approach this situation very cautiously,"* he admonished.

Killibrew moved out; I followed closely behind. Nearing the camp, I heard what sounded like a small radio playing country and Western music. Putting a finger to his lips, Killibrew signaled quiet! He said softly, *"Cover me."* A pistol in one hand, he parted the flap where the door came together. Peeping through the split, he held up two fingers, indicating there were two people inside. He quietly stepped through the flap. I could see a small light dimly illuminating their tent. Killibrew moved closer. He placed his gun against the man's cheek. The man jumped as Killibrew grabbed his neck with his other hand. His movement woke the woman.

It was an elderly couple. Frightened, the old white

guy scanned the camper as though looking for an opportunity to pull some stunt out of his ass. Catching his eyes as they rushed past, they reflected panic and desperation. He was powerless. Under such circumstances and in the presence of white women, white guys can lose it entirely. I'd seen that look on a few previous occasions. It was the look in that guy's eyes just before T-ball blew his brains out in that bank. Killibrew must have seen it too in Billy Bob's eyes when he slit his throat.

This old guy was like any white man staring up the business end of a gun held by a black man. There isn't any worst position for a white man to get caught, and it makes them panicky.

White women know this too. So, when Killibrew said, "I don't want to kill you, and you don't want to die. If you don't do anything to make me hurt you, you don't have to worry about dying. I could have killed you as you slept if I wanted you dead. So listen carefully. Answer my questions truthfully. And this will be over quickly. Do you have a first-aid kit?"

The woman answered quickly, "Yes, it's over there. It

is in one of those packs."

"Good." Trenchant, Killibrew still held the man down with his left hand around his neck and the gun resting on his nose. He asked, "Do you have any food?"

The woman pointed to a table as she answered. "In those bags, and there is some in the cooler." She reached over and clutched the old guy's hand as she answered. It was as if she knew he was trying to think of something stupid to do, which would have made a bad situation even worse.

"Do you have cell phones?" Killibrew continued his inventory.

"On the table." Answering, she released the old guy's hand, reached under his pillow, took out a cell phone and a small caliber handgun, and handed them in Killibrew's direction. I took them in my free hand. The old guy looked at her as though she had just betrayed him.

Killibrew thanked her, then looked at the old guy and said, *"She probably saved your life.*

You should thank her too." The old guy simply lay there with a blank expression on his face.

Observing Killibrew, I learned an important lesson. The key to control is dominance. Control depends on whether and how expected trouble spots are anticipated. And neutralizing or mitigating them is the challenge. This is why things fell apart for my boys and me in that bank. We didn't look in the direction from which problems were most likely to come. We didn't anticipate it. Holding the old guy down without any chance of him moving, Killibrew didn't have to watch him. He could concentrate on why we were there, and most importantly, the old guy knew he would be the first to die.

"Now comes the tricky part," Killibrew said, looking at the old guy as he released his grip on his neck. *"You are going to come with me outside and unhook the truck from the camper. While we do that, the Mrs. is going to redress my friend's wound. After that, we will leave you, good people, just as we found you, minus a few things I'm sure you'll be glad to live without. Is that clear?"* Killibrew directed his question toward the

woman.

"Yes," she replied, then got to her feet, walked over to the packs, and retrieved the first aid kit. Turning and looking at the old guy, who was still lying in bed looking as if he was going to try some cowboy shit at any moment, she asked, *"Aren't you going to put on your rain gear, honey? You don't want to catch your death out there in all of that rain, do you? They are over here in your pack. You hadn't forgotten where you put them, had you?"* With that, she turned to me and said, *"Now, let me see if I can help you."* Her face was adorned with a smile that said she knew she had successfully negotiated their safety.

It was nearing sunrise when we made it to the main road. Luckily, there were several maps in the truck. With them, we were able to avoid the highway while searching for a thickly wooded area that would conceal the truck. Still fighting a constant downpour, we found the perfect spot on a crest overlooking the road and a creek, with trees and large boulders for cover. We ate and then took turns napping. It was still raining and near dark when we pulled out. Killibrew headed southward towards the

Blue Ridge Mountains through West Virginia.

He said, *"I believe it's best to stay in the mountains, lest traffic. That route is longer, but after that run-in with the Ohio cop, going south is our only option. "* Killibrew rubbed his chin and said, *"Mexico was where we sent those on the run that couldn't get into Canada. My Spanish is rusty, but we've run out of options."*

We crossed a bridge that spanned the rain-swollen Jackson River. The rushing water in the rain-swollen river was eroding its bank while sucking trees and anything else along its showers into it. Again, Killibrew talked as we rode. Sometime later, I realized he was shaking me. I opened my eyes. I'd dozed off at some point.

"We got trouble. There's a roadblock around the bend. I can see headlights through the trees. This truck is probably on their hot sheet by now, so I'm not going to try and bullshit our way past them."

The cops at the roadblock must have spotted Killibrew turning the truck around. Lights on patrol cars, which were already flashing, started moving.

Speeding away as Killibrew turned the truck around, some troopers at the roadblock immediately gave chase and some began shooting. With lights flashing, sirens blaring, and guns blazing, they were on us like a hound after a rabbit.

Killibrew was flying down the road while looking for a turnoff. Suddenly the rear window shattered. I felt the same burning, stinging agony I felt running from the raid at Unidyn when that bullet ripped into my side. The pain was in my shoulder and lower leg this time. My body lunged forward from the impact. Blood spattered the front windshield, and I looked over at Killibrew. I could see blood covering his shirt. Though hit pretty badly, he continued driving. Killibrew seemed to be gritting his teeth; for some reason, he reminded me of a bulldog.

Firing as they gave chase, the troopers in hot pursuit from the roadblock were gaining on us. I stuck the automatic out of the hole in the shattered back window and started firing as Killibrew sped on. I saw one patrol car leave the road in a tumble, which caused another to flip and cartwheel off to the other side. Killibrew took the first turnoff he saw. We had no time to look at maps; we were running for our lives. I felt I was in better shape to drive than Killibrew, but we didn't have time to switch. So, he drove, and I fired out the back as we rode.

Going as fast as the rain-slick road, hills, and curves allowed, Killibrew didn't look like he had any quick maneuvers in his bag of tricks that could shake five patrol cars. We came up a hill. Killibrew around a bend, with the Smith Bridge down in the valley and another roadblock. Killibrew slowed to a stop. He looked at me and said, "Well, kid, it's been a great ride. "This is it, kid. Hold on!"

All I could say was, "Thanks for everything." Amazingly, during that moment, looking over at Killibrew, the image of my father flashed in my head, and then I understood my mother's admonition about him. Now, I understand what it means to spend time in the presence of a man.

Killibrew started down the hill at normal speed. The cars chasing us rounded the curve just as we reached halfway. Killibrew floored the gas pedal, and the big truck roared. Shifting gears with the precision of a surgeon yet clutching with the accuracy of a jeweler, the big truck lunged and sped forward. It seemed to take mere seconds for the truck to reach top speed. Simultaneously, cops at the roadblock took cover behind vehicles and began firing. They soon realized bullets couldn't stop the big truck headed straight for them; they scattered.

Flying at top speed, the truck rammed the roadblock. There was a huge explosion that sent patrol cars flying. We must have looked like the main attraction in a real live demolition derby. Flames and smoke were everywhere. Plowing through the roadblock of cars, the truck became airborne. The railing on the bridge caught the truck's back wheels as it flew through the air. Flipping over as it soared, even with a seatbelt on, I felt like a marble rolling around in a matchbox. My only thought as we plunged into the river was of Nate and Goose tumbling down into that ravine after that crash in New Jersey. It seemed I was finally about to join them. I knew it was all over when the truck slammed into the river and filled with water almost immediately.

The next thing I knew, I was being swept along by the

fast-moving current of the rain-swollen river, entangled in the branches or roots of a fallen tree. I had bemoaned the rain since we ran into it in the Poconos. However, the rain-swollen river, which was out of its banks, became a soft-landing rather than the usual rocky shoreline. Caught in its branches, a dead tree saved my life. Unconscious until that moment, surely I would have drowned were it not for the log. Surviving my second fiery crash, I wondered how I got out of the truck. Confused and dazed but grateful I was safe, as a previous question returned. *Why me?*

I thought about Killibrew and wondered if Providence had intervened on his behalf too. I survived so Killibrew could have also. He was much tougher than I'll ever be. Thinking about our ordeal together, I felt he'd helped me grow up. Now, I understood some of the real facts of life. I'd been around. I'd gone to the school of hard knocks. I'd beaten my head against the Ivy walls at the University of Last Chances and Hard Knocks and graduated Magna cun Laude. So, I wasn't a dummy. After majoring in staying alive, I thought I was a pretty smart guy. But Killibrew showed me I had learned Jackshit, only lots of details and facts. That only meant I was smart enough to get my ass into lots of trouble, not how to get it out, as my current screw-up proves. Putting it together, I didn't know shit! After three and a half days with Killibrew, I'd learned more about life than all my years of schooling combined. I had no idea what life held for me going forward, but because of Killibrew, I knew a better man would face it. No matter what it was!

Chapter V:

A Clueless Companion

Momentarily disoriented when I awoke, my heart raced, after reliving the nightmare escape with Killibrew from Unidyn and the plunge into the river. Fully awake, I realized I was back safe in the cabin. Lying on the rug, I had slept the day away. I must have been exhausted—my adrenalin must have been truly pumping.

The fire had died, and already there was a chill in the air. Even on late summer evenings, the atmosphere cools rapidly. Once the sun retreated behind the mountains, I never wanted to allow the fire to die. I liked keeping the place nice and toasty. Astonished, I would sleep so long, I tossed a few logs in the fireplace, I woozily watched the coals set them ablaze.

Darkness also comes quickly once the sun disappears

behind the mountains, so I turned on a small light in the hallway. Dreamily haunting thoughts of my unconscious houseguest, lingered in my head like morning fog in the low country. I checked on Miss Madison Avenue, hoping things had changed, but her comatose state continued. Replacing the cold pack, which had fallen off during the night and melted, I checked her vitals to confirm she hadn't expired. Everything seemed normal.

After warming soup and bread, I settled down at the table. Thinking about the previous day's excitement, I realized I hadn't eaten anything other than cereal and fruit before going for my run. Although calmness, peace, and quiet are desirable around here, the thoughts of my lovely house guest added a little spice to my otherwise bland existence. Unwanted as she was, my heart hadn't pounded so much from thoughts of a woman since Doreen.

I heard a groaning sound and turned in the direction of her bed. Eating my second large bowl of soup, I expected nothing more than to replace the cold compress. But a big smile spread across my face, revealing my pleasure of seeing her sitting up in bed, wide-eyed with an amazed expression on her face. The sudden change in her condition made greeting her, like a kid opening Christmas presents, "Well, hello! Good to see you finally came around! Are you all right?" Confident a full explanation of her unfortunate circumstances would now be forthcoming, smiling, I waited calmly.

Clutching the blanket before her as though hiding her nudity, she screamed, "What the hell is this? Who are you? Where am I? How did I get here?"

Her questions regarding 'who' and 'how,' I understood, but the 'where' I wasn't sure was about her location. I thought she'd missed the point of my greeting, which was a prelude to her telling me how she happened to be in the mountains alone. Confused, I felt I was the one who should be asking that question. Moreover, I figured her 'where' pertained to the cabin not the general area. Also, I noticed a wildly hysterical look in her eyes that wasn't there back on the trail. The upshot to me was I had no idea where this was going.

Now, it seemed that the startled reaction I expected back on the trail was about to explode into a full-blown panic attack. I tried to preempt that, "Hold on! Settle down! I'm not going to harm you. I found you just before you passed out on the trail yesterday."

"Yesterday! You've had me here since yesterday!" Her screaming continued, seemingly getting edgier with every word.

"Lady, you passed out on the trail before you told me anything. What was I supposed to do? Leave you out there alone and unconscious?"

Moving around in the bed as though looking for an exit, she questioned loudly, "Passed out? What trail? If I passed out, why didn't you carry me to the hospital? How do I know you aren't a kidnapper or a psycho of some sort? What kind of place is this anyway?"

Unsure what to say to calm her down, I said, "Lady, you're out in the middle of nowhere, not in the city! You don't remember anything from our meeting on the trail?"

Acting even more panicky, she repeated her earlier question, "Where am I?"

"You're in my cabin. It's not too far from where I found you." I knew her blood pressure was going through the roof when she jumped to her feet and grabbed the African souvenir spear displayed on the wall above the bed, and pointed it in my direction.

I was right. Her blood had rushed to her head. Jumping to her feet after lying down for two days, her equilibrium was shot.

Looking around, after standing up, she took a few wobbly steps in the bed. Hearing the shakiness of her voice, then saw the wobble of her knees and recognized it all, as a prelude to her performance back on the trail. "How did I get here-e-e-e-e?" I moved to catch her just as she dropped the spear and tumbled head first headed for the floor. Jumping while turning over on my back, I slid beneath her. Catching her body in mid-air just before she hit the floor, my quick move prevented her from landing headfirst. Her lights had gone out again.

I put her back in bed and covered her with the blanket. My mind raced back to the first day I awoke in the same bed, after Jordan brought me here. Only there wasn't anyone around to catch me and prevent me from banging my head as I fell to the floor. Fortunately, I was standing on the floor rather than standing up in the bed like her. My fall nearly cost me my life as it was.

She had gone off like a rocket. Wondering how she would have reacted to being undressed in the steam room was no longer a question. The situation would have gotten totally out of hand. Never considering she would be so edgy, I was unprepared for her becoming hysterical. I had no idea my face would be so frightening at first glance. Maybe it was the beard. I don't know.

It was understandable that she would be confused and disoriented, waking up in a strange place and finding a strange man looking at her, but I never thought she would respond as though she was a prisoner. What could have caused her to react so strangely? As Jordan would say: *The irony here is you are like a man in a river, standing with each foot on a different log and with no way to keep them from drifting apart. That's a situation that must be handled very delicately, or you will end up wet all over.*

I must approach her differently when she regains consciousness, or this could get very ugly. My dilemma had only worsened. Not only are her identity and reason for being in the mountains still mysteries, but their threat has also increased. Having seen me here, in this cabin, when she opened her eyes, the only way out now is to move her before she regains consciousness. Keeping her here wasn't part of the plan, but where do I carry her?

Rushing to the laundry room to get our clothes from the dryer, I mulled over the situation. I thought as I went back to her bed: *The first thing was to get her into something other than a shirt without any panties. That was certainly not how she needed to find herself once she was awakens.* I thought returning from the laundry room: *Maybe, regaining consciousness doesn't mean everything will be fine if and when she comes around again.* Laying the clothes on a chair and pulling back the blanket, I slipped her into her panties. My thoughts continued racing wildly: *She needed to be kept calm, and I had to be ready to deliver her to any place she wanted to go as soon as she opened her eyes. I couldn't afford to have the police poking around. If that happens, Jordan's worst fears will become my living nightmare.* Under these circumstances, there isn't a worse scenario to envision.

Under pressure, I convenced myself I was thinking like Jordan. S*trike while the iron is hot! Move her while she's still unconscious. Put her in the truck, drive her into the valley, and dump her on someone else's doorstep before she realizes where she is.*

Ambivalent and confused, my panicky thoughts grew desperate: *Self-preservation is the best thing. All I needed to do was get rid of her, put her off on someone else, or in someplace she will be easily found.*

The more I thought, the deeper into quicksand I felt myself sinking. Now, worse than flypaper, this reminded me of that old Uncle Remus fable, *Brer Rabbit and Tar Baby*. Once it's touched, you can never get free of its tar.

As I reached for her clothes, preparing to dress her, the sight of her beautiful legs sticking from beneath the oversized T-shirt triggered memories of my reaction to her enticing body in the steam chamber; I paused. *What if the person who finds her lacks restraint? I had some erotic thoughts while washing and touching her, but those were only thoughts so I stopped. Dumping her helpless body out someplace just to get rid of her would be abandoning her to the real possibility a pervert or fiend of some kind may find her. Even if they are good people and deliver her to a hospital or authorities, there is no way to know what will happen to her without identification. Then, whatever happens to her will be my fault. I will have placed her in even worse danger than leaving her back on the trail.*

What to do? I was back wrestling with the same old dilemma, trying to figure out what to do with a strange unconscious woman I now felt obligated to protect. Stepping away from the bed, I sat on a stool at the bar as my thoughts continued. *Maybe to the detriment of Archangel, and myself, I had become a prisoner of this unknown unconscious woman who believed she was my prisoner.* There seemed to be no way out of this paradox for me.

Suddenly, she popped up in bed, making all my questions moot. Awakening with a wide eyed deer in the headlights stare, she scanned the room as if she wanted to make a break for the door but didn't see one.

Quickly trying to reassure her that she was in no danger, I said, *"Please, lady, give me a chance to explain. Honestly, I mean you no harm. If I was a kidnapper or a psycho of some kind, I would have tied up, especially after trying to skewer me with that spear. I left it by the bed where you dropped it, just in case it made you feel safer."*

Glancing down, she grabbed the spear, picking it up, she pointed in my direction. I continued trying calmly to explain the situation. *"I know you are confused as I am. I didn't ask for any of this. Stumbling upon you on the trail, I thought you were a lost camper. Looking around, however, there wasn't a campsite near where I saw you, and you didn't have a backpack, medical bracelet, or any other kind of identification. So, when you passed out, what was I supposed to do other than bring you home with me? I'm sure you didn't want me to leave you out on the trail unconscious in a forest filled with snakes and bears, did you?"* I had never seen a bear in these parts, but she couldn't have known that.

My questions and statements mollified her. Still moving uneasily in the bed, she looked at the place as though searching for a response. Finally, "N-n-no-o-o-o-o," stammered out.

Her stammering admission seemed to ease her anxiety. Gradually, she lowered the spear, as she let it fall to the floor, conceding my point that she wasn't in any danger. She still looked dazed but no longer afraid, so I thought I would seize the initiative. *"Lady! Who are you? What's your name? How did you get out here alone? Is there someone you want me to contact or someplace you want to be taken?"*

Almost without hesitation, she began to speak but stopped in mid-sentence. *"My name is...."* a confused expression covered her face. She repeated, "My name is."

"Yes, go on," I encouraged. Her confusion grew as she struggled to say her name. The wild look on her face reminded me of the last time she passed out. Watching her struggle, I sensed that might have been her problem before, but then her confusion was general. Now, my question demanded something specific, her name. Panic ensued. She repeated the same phrase as though stuck in rewind, *"My name is ah-h-h. My name is ah-ah-ah-*

ah. My name ah-ah-ah-h-h-h."

Rapidly, she repeated those same words as though saying them would produce a different answer. Tears flooded her eyes as she blurted out. "I don't know my name! What have you done to me? Why don't I know who I am? Why don't I remember my name?"

Frightened, she reached down and picked up the spear again. Holding it as though warding off an attacker, she pointed it at me. It was not a threatening gesture. It seemed a demand for personal space or a need to buy time while the reality of the situation settled in. So, I moved away from her, raising my hands with the palms showing.

Up on her knees in the bed, she moved around like a frightened caged animal. I stepped behind the breakfast bar to give her a sense of security. Finally, her frightened eyes settled on mine. Not wanting to lose eye contact, I didn't blink. She seemed to be searching for something to trust. I could hear her breathing across the room. Stillness came over her as she settled into a motionless stare. Our eyes locked on one another. It was as though we were holding each other in an embrace.

It seemed time was riding on the back of a snail. We watched one another, not moving, frozen as the seconds crept. The world around us disappeared as a reality. That moment became the world for both of us, like a lifeline to reality. What it would become would be determined by what happened from that moment forward. I knew the next move was mine, as our eyes remained locked on one another.

Finally tears that had trickled down her cheeks began flowing freely; she broke down completely. Quietly and slowly, so as not to frighten her, I knew she needed consoling. Gradually, I moved towards her. She didn't move away. I extended my arms, but again she didn't move away. Easing closer, I placed my arm around her shoulders. Pulling her head onto my chest, we embraced as she sobbed wildly.

"What has happened to me? Why don't I know who I am? How could I not remember my name?" Her questions came amidst heavy sobbing. I continued holding her, without words, as she boohooed. Her last questions no longer blamed me for her condition, which gave me an opening. So, I continued holding her,

encouraging her to stop crying, *"There, there now. Don't cry. Don't cry. We'll figure this out. It will be alright."* I sensed her desperate struggle to compose herself. Maybe she felt vulnerable and out of control, but gradually she stopped crying.

With that opening, I'd hoped to move beyond the moment. I spoke calmly, *"Let me get you a drink of water. You must be thirsty. A parched throat can make it difficult to talk and think."* I went to the refrigerator, got water, removed the top, and handed the bottle to her. Taking the water very quickly, she spilled a little. Gulping it down nonstop, I pulled the bottle away, spilling a little more. I cautioned, *"Take it easy! You'll make yourself sick! Just a little at a time."* She looked at me strangely; her face had a puzzled expression.

I gave her the water again. That seemed to calm her, and the anxious look faded. So I volunteered, "You asked several questions earlier because of your attair I didn't know what to think. I had no way of knowing who you are and how you got out here, but I can tell you where you are. We're just South of the Shenandoah National Forest, East of the West Virginia state line in Allegheny

County, Virginia, and North of the Roanoke Gap section of the Blue Ridge Mountains. They call where w are Lake Moomaw-Gathright Dam reservoir, but this cabin is about twenty-five miles up in the mountains—about 3200 feet.

We're so high up and off the beaten path only true outdoor lovers, like hikers, backpackers, bikers, bird watchers, and nature enthusiasts, venture this far up. That's why when I saw you dressed as you were, I thought you were sightseeing and had gotten separated from your party. I looked around, but there wasn't another soul anywhere. Standing on a hill watching you, I was confused. That's why I decided to come over and ask if you needed help.

Thinking you were lost, I could provide directions. I approached you to ask if you needed help, but before you gave me any information you passed out. Do you remember anything about being out here or how you got here? Can you remember ever being out here before?"

She only shook her head, giving a negative response to my questions. The faraway look in her eyes mimicked her overall detachment from her situation. She looked as if she had no connection to any of this. *"You were wearing these clothes when I stumbled upon you."* I turned and picked up her things from the chair beside the bed.

"As you can see, it isn't the typical attire for a girl's day out in the woods, particularly those shoes. Does any of this ring a bell?"

Taking the clothes, she looked as though they were a total enigma. She said, Are you sure these are mine? I don't wear these kinds of clothes you must have me mixed up with another person. Then, she looked at the oversized T-shirt she was wearing. Pulling it out at the hemline, she asked, "Who does this belong to and how did I come to have this on?"

Sheepishly, I said, "Well, when I stumbled upon you, your clothes had mud and stuff covering them. So I undressed you, and like your clothes, your body needed washing, so I gave you a quick shower, but I kept my eyes closed." I couldn't bring myself to tell her about how dirty she was and where I washed her up for fear that may cause further questioning of my motives.

My clumsy attempt at humor may not have gone over well, but it did cover up my real guilt. She responded to it all, with a deadpan, "I bet you did." We both chuckle briefly. That interlude broke the iciness and warmed the atmosphere a bit. I continued my offensive, *"You must be starving. It has been at least two days since you've eaten anything because you have been here a full day and a half without a bite."*

She recoiled as if trying to remember the last time she had food. She confessed, *"I don't remember the last time I ate."*

"There's a fire going, but if you're cold, you can get into your things or the pants I laid on the foot of the bed. The bathroom is at the end of the hall if you want to change." I pointed in its direction as I spoke.

I didn't think she was cool, but I wanted her to feel comfortable, and knowing I was concerned about her comfort could ease her apprehension. Having on pants in the presence of a strange man should help her relax in such an odd situation. As I talked, she picked up the pants and stepped down the hallway to the bathroom; the door closed behind her.

Chapter VI:

Goodnight Jericho

After a while she emerged from the bathroom wearing my baggy pants and the oversized shirt, looking like someone from the rumpled saggy hip hop world from which she came. *"Come have a seat here at the table where you can be comfortable eating. Yesterday I made soup and herb bread and there's ginger tea also. but if you are a meat eater, you are up the creek around here. I'm strictly vegetarian,"* I informed her proudly.

Surprisingly, she countered, *"Me too! My girlfriend Margie and I got off the meat wagon almost a year ago."*

"Margie! Who's Margie?"

"A girlfriend from work."

"Yeah? Where do you work?"

"I work at....."

She stopped mid-sentence again.

"I don't remember."

She said wearing a confused grimace

"Well, tell me some more about Margie."

"I don't remember any more about her"

"What's the last memory you have before waking up here?" "That's it. Waking up here."

"You don't remember anything about yourself before today?" "No"

"Do you have a mental picture of anything from your past?"

"No! No! No! Can't you see? I don't remember anything! What do you want me to do, makeup something?"

"Okay! Okay! It's alright." I could see she was tensing up. *"I'm sorry if I seemed to be pressing you. Your*

situation is so unusual. We don't have to talk about you anymore. You can just enjoy your meal. For dessert, I have homemade wild berry and nut muffins."

I got a large bowl from the cabinet, filled it with soup, and placed a thick slice of bread in front of her. Before I could get her a spoon, she broke off a piece of bread and dunked it into the soup.

"Be careful. It is hot!" I cautioned.

She took the spoon without comment. Blowing, slurping, and dunking, the bowl of soup seemed to vanish within minutes.

So as not to embarrass her, I volunteered, *"Here, let me get you a little more."*

While I got more soup, she continued munching on the bread. As soon as my hands cleared the bowl, she dove back into her blowing, slurping, and dunking routine. I watched her, amazed, and I was unable to eat myself. It was obvious she had not eaten in days. Suspiciously at first, I thought *it was not too difficult to fake amnesia, but hunger is another matter altogether.* The way she went at that hot soup left no doubt. I hoped she wasn't burning her mouth raw.

I thought I'd keep it light, so I opened with, *"I'm not a very good soup and bread man. What do you think?"*

<u>"Uh, hun!"</u> She mumbled. *"This is very good.*

She said between scoops of soup and bites of bread.

I thought her posture resembled a cave dweller. Crouched over the bowl, head down, arms raised with her elbows sticking out parallel to her shoulders, head bowed, spoon in one hand and bread in the other, there wasn't any doubt of her prolonged lack of nourishment. Observing her eating, my suspicion of her being an agent lessened because, in my book, only something as severe as near starvation could make such an attractive woman behave so piggishly in front of a man.

Almost finished with her third bowl, she must have sensed me watching her. Stopping abruptly, she moved her eyes upward on me before I could look away. When I did, it made observing her all the more obvious. Embarrassed, I repeated my earlier offer. *"I-I-I have wild berry and nut muffins for dessert.*

I'll get you some."

"You're repeating yourself, and yes, I would love some." Her response was as quick as a trapdoor falling. *Why did I feel out-maneuvered?* She was munching on her last piece of bread as I placed a saucer with three miniature muffins before her. She grabbed two. Gobbling one, she held the other at the ready while she chewed. Unable to look away the entire time she ate, I realized being the center of my focus may have made her feel uncomfortable, but her hunger took precedence.

Consuming the third muffin, she stated matter-of-factly, *"I slept with you last night."* Her effort trying to smile was an indication her statement was a jest. *"Or, in your bed, that is, and I don't even know your name."* She smiled shyly. *"What's your *name?"*

Trying to buy time while I decided how to handle this question, I said, *"Hasn't your mother told you not to talk with your mouth full?"* The shake-and-bake stall may have bought me time, but it drew a stiff defense.

Swallowing quickly, defensively, she slid over my dribble side. It seemed she liked wordplay. So, like a basketball player, she slid over to my dribble hand. *"My momma always said good conversation helps your digestion."*

I tried a crossover move, *"What's your mother's name?"*

"Ada, but I call her momma."

She backed off and waited for me to drive. So I threw up a long shot. *"Do you live with her?"*

"No. She lives in Richmond; I live in DC." She beat me to the rebound.

"But we aren't supposed to talk about me, and you still haven't told me your name." She cut off my move to the baseline, so I gave up the ball.

Less convinced of the agent scenario, I said, *"It's Richard Kirksey, but my boys call me Jericho."* Watching closely for an attempt to block my shot, I looked for a reaction to a name I believed most government agents should be familiar with; she simply kept her eyes on the ball.

"Do you live here with your family?" She began her side out by driving straight to the basket for a quick lay-up.

"No, I don't have a family."

She cut off my drive by stealing the ball.

"Well, do you have a mother?

Refusing to concede the point, I bumped her off stride with my reply. *"I live alone, and my mother passed away when I was very young,"* I was sure my backdoor move would get around her with a head fake.

"I'm sorry to hear that." She conceded the game.

"Don't be. That was a long time ago." Even though I made my point, I didn't feel like a winner. I thought: Maybe my apprehension and paranoia caused me to overshoot the goal. Normally cutting off the conversation so bluntly may be a good strategy, but under these circumstances, I needed to keep her talking. She may have revealed more information about herself. I must be careful the next time we are engaged in wordplay; I need to let the game flow to unravel this mystery.

Following that exchange, silence replaced my probing. Her dessert finished, she requested a glass of juice. I poured a big one, and she drank it nonstop.

She seemed satiated, so I said, "Dinner seems completed, so let us adjoin to the living area. We settled down by the fireplace. Not wanting to pressure her for information, our silence continued. I watched her fidget. She wrung her hands, while constantly changing positions, shifting from sitting upright to leaning back on the sofa, then sprawling cat-like before the fire and curling up into a fetal-like knot.

I tried to imagine what it must be like to be alone in an isolated forest, a stranger to myself, and dependent on the good intentions of a strange man. *Could I be trusted? What were my real motives? Had her situation happened the way I said?* I believed these questions were swirling in her head. It reminded me of my reaction the first time I woke up after Jordan brought me here. And the panic attack that followed. And I didn't have amnesia.

Cautiously, I suggested, "Why not watch the news? There may be a missing person's report out on you. I'm sure your family or someone has missed you by now. If there isn't anything on TV, you can go online. There are lots of sites that list people missing all over the country." I thought, *Maybe having unfettered access to a computer would relieve more of her anxiety and make her feel less like a prisoner. Open communication with the outside world could relieve her uneasiness since the police were just a click away.* My suggestion broke her silence.

"Yeah, great, I would like that!" She responded enthusiastically.

"While you're doing that, I will take care of some things outside before I lie down for the night."

The smile that followed my suggestion indicated she felt I was concerned about her predicament. That may lessen her anxiety even more.

She continued to smile, but her anxious look faded. She asked, "So you have a computer? I love working with computers. They make research so much easier. Don't you think?"

I started to pursue her remark, remembering she liked working with computers and research, but I decided to answer the question and let her thoughts flow to see if she would say more. I replied, *"Yes."*

"What kind of system do you have?" she asked.

"A Mac, with major modifications, it's over there on the table." I pointed to a darkened corner in an unlit portion of the room.

"Yeah! Macs are great. Where I work, there are only PCs run on Microsoft."

Her voice dropped as though she suddenly remembered her amnesia. I turned on The TV and pretended not to notice how her comments about work seemed to shut her reminiscing down. Why did talking about work produce such tension and create a memory block? Is work involved in her memory loss? Could that be the reason she's here? What kind of job would bring a beautiful woman out in the woods dressed in street clothes, other than some type of investigator? I thought *Cooper John would say, this girl has a story to tell. And I'm listening.*

Preparing to go outside, I offered. "There's fresh coffee on the stove if you want some. Cups are in the cupboard on the right."

Hearing a familiar sound and turning to investigate, I noticed she had quietly moved to the computer and turned it on, leaving the TV to entertain itself. Sometimes, I like having it as background noise too. She may be the same and might have responded to some deep psychological urge to have something familiar happening.

I put on a jacket and hat before starting to the door. Opening it, I looked back at her before closing it behind me. I could see her eyes following me across the room. Those bright orbs reminded me of that look you see in a dog's eyes when you leave it behind. *Will I ever see you again if you disappear from my sight kind of look?* You know the one. I wanted to reassure her, but like the dog, you can't carry it with you every time you leave. So, I closed the door behind me as I stepped onto the porch.

Oh, quit it! I can't stand it anymore. You are about to make me sick with that sympathetic dribble. Jordan's admonitions reverberated in my head like sound bouncing off cave walls. *Here you go again, all tied up in knots over a stray puppy. What if she isn't who she is pretending to be? If I told you once, I've told you a hundred times you can't go soft when some helpless Jane shows up on your doorstep. You don't believe all this memory loss bullshit, do you? That's the oldest trick in the book. That way, she doesn't have to make sense or keep her story straight. You should have left her on the trail, and you wouldn't have to...*

Ah, come on, Jordan. My internal battle continued. *You can't be seriously suggesting what I think you are. That just isn't right! Look at her! She doesn't seem to be faking. I have to play along with this until I can figure out what her real game is, if she has one. If things aren't as she's pretending they are, what does that mean? If you're right, I need to know how much she knows about me. Who sent her, and how did they find me?*

You did one hell of a job concealing this place. You've hidden out here for over twenty years, and nobody even got close to tracking you down. And you've done far more damage than I have or will ever do. This is about far more than whether or not she's faking memory loss. If this is a game, where did I go wrong to lead them here? I haven't left the mountains in four months.

When I undressed her, I gave her clothes the once over, and there were no tracking devices. I used the handheld to check her for implants. She's clean. No, if she was sent in, they are playing for more than just me.

I grabbed a pair of night vision goggles from a case Jordan kept in the back of his truck and went up to my favorite place where I sit and think. Climbing the rock face that covers the back of the cabin, I continued musing about my lovely house guest.

After reaching the top of the rocky ledge that overhangs the cabin, I marveled to myself at how reassuring it is to settle down in my favorite spot. It's the perfect place when there's a need to be certain there aren't any strange movements or flyovers. The only way anyone could track her if she's an agent is by satellite, which means they know her location.

Continuing to muse, I thought about Jordan's hideout's strategic setting. This position offers a clear view of the valley below and all approaches to the cabin; it's virtually impossible to approach without being seen. The lush ground cover conceals an elaborate observation and warning system. Cameras and sensing devices covered the mountainside. Jordan designed the system using wireless digital miniature transmitters/receivers that can be checked and activated from any location, anywhere. But I'm old-fashion; personal observation always add a greater sense of security for me.

The road approaching the cabin comes up from the valley, out of the woods, and divides. The right driveway goes down the side. In contrast, the left drive comes up across the front of the cabin. Built where the land slopes upward and flattens out back towards the rock face and toward the edge of a cliff, A garage and tool shed flanked the South side of the cabin. A walkway runs from the steam chamber to the front steps. The huge rock face that runs a half-mile into the forest serves as a back fence. Jordan cleared the trees and underbrush away, so the lawn extends from the drive 60 yards to the woods and over to my vegetable garden at the edge cliff.

Jordan couldn't have chosen a better defensive position. The monitoring devices and onscreen viewing allow for surveilling everything on monitors inside the cabin. But I like visual observation—I hate trusting machines.

There is something about sitting up here, atop everything, and looking down on the world. Sometimes, I sit up here for hours. The nights are quiet and peaceful, stars twinkling above, and when the moon's full, it lights up the valley almost as bright as day. Satisfied no one was sneaking around outside or buzzing the place from on high, I climbed down from the ledge. After more than an hour, I returned to the cabin. Opening the door, she turned away from the computer and greeted me with a smile. The fireplace lit up her face, casting an orange glow upon it. Her eyes reflected the flickering flames as

the computer screen created an eerie bluish backdrop in the darkened corner of the room. *"You're back!"* She let out a sigh as though she had been holding her breath ever

since the door closed behind me. Her eyes sparkled, and the flicker of flames from the fire's reflection on her dark skin triggered a vague recollection. Perhaps, it was a dream or a forgotten moment strangely like this one that her presence rekindled. The firelight dancing in her eyes cast a familiar glow that lit up a dark place in my heart, which had been covered over by cobwebs, dust, and shadows. But, the reflection died quickly, like an ember from a blaze, so my brain wasn't able to identify it before the fleeting engram faded.

It was as if I had seen that look someplace before. How could that be? We have never met. Then again, those big glowing orbs flashing brightly from her darkly shadowed face were all too real to me. In that brief moment, I experienced such a familiar sensation. But we had never seen each other before, or had we? I wanted to ask the question aloud, but her amnesia wouldn't allow her to answer, even if we had. So, I asked instead, "Have any luck?"

Her eyes lowered as she slowly turned her face back to the computer again. *"N-no-o-o,"* she offered reluctantly.

An apprehensive gaze had already replaced the comfortable smile and bright dancing eyes. It was as if my question pulled her back to her present reality from someplace, much like the one I had gone, when the need to ask the question nearly overwhelmed me. Taking off my jacket and hat, I noticed how comfortably she sat at the computer. She didn't ask for any assistance or operating instructions, which to me meant she was doing something she's done before and lots of times.

Being comfortable with computers, to some extent, is probably how some people feel about pets. They talk to them. I, on the other hand, don't have nor do I desire intimate knowledge of computers. I consider them tools, like pencils or library cards. Techies or technogeeks are cool. I know some people who eat, drink and sleep that stuff. Doreen was that way. She talked about computers as though they were the *second coming*. Me, I never even learned to program a VCR

This stranger seemed to fall into Doreen's category. Looking at her, she exhibited some classic signs. Based on personal observations, I believe people who work with computers often develop little idiosyncrasies they probably never notice. The way they sit in their chairs. The way they hold their bodies and their way of slumping after working for hours. Where they place things, like pins, paper, and coffee cups, the tilt of their monitors, and the placement of the mouse and keyboard, are all little subtleties that creep in as work habits the longer they sit at a computer. And, from where I stood, I could see my workstation change the longer she sat at the console. I decided to try my ultimate test for computer geeks.

I asked matter-of-factly, "How about another cup of coffee? You look as if you'll be there a while." Without turning her head away from the screen, she picked up her cup and pushed it in my direction.

"Sure! You know, I had no idea so many people turn up missing under all kinds of circumstances. Some are never found or heard from again." Her voice dropped on that note as though she remembered she was one of those people.

Hurrying with the coffee to break her somber train of thought, I said, "Here's your coffee."

"Thank you," she said. Never turning her head, she placed the cup in the same spot from where she retrieved it, proving my point.

Although her smile dimmed, her eyes lit up my mind with burning thoughts and that familiar question, *had I drowned in her gaze somewhere before?* Considering how relaxed she worked when I was outside, I thought she might do better alone if she continued.

The tendency of computer jocks and researchers to snack while working may kick in, so I offered. "I have food in the fridge, and snacks are in the pantry if you get hungry. Extra blankets in the closet under the stairs if you need them. I'm going to bed; the day hasn't been long. But I feel drained; it must be fatigue from yesterday. My bed is up at the head of the stairs, so if you need me, just give me a shout. I'm a very light sleeper. I'll see you in the morning. Goodnight!"

Goodnight Jericho! The soft sweet sound of her voice saying goodnight was like a giant steam shovel excavating the caverns in my memory, dredging up old feelings and experiences long since buried within the recesses of my closed mind.

Chapter VII:

Thy Brother's Keeper

Opening my eyes, the next morning, with a prayer that our efforts bring greater clarity to my confused house guest, as I began day three. I felt good about how things had gone and my actions were proper and guided by Godly love. Once out of bed, going for my morning jog was the highlight of my day. But her presence made me decide to stay close. I didn't want her to wake up unable to find me easily. Considering breakfast, I thought, *Some fresh berries would be nice.* Strawberry, mulberry, dewberry, blueberry, and blackberry seasons ended in late spring or mid-summer. Only raspberries were available until cranberry season began in late summer into early fall. Berries are delightful with granola and rice milk. One of my duties at Archangel is to check the security fence. Sometimes a sensor goes off or some other malfunctions. During those tours, I discovered most of my berry caches.

Great natural foods are easy to get in the Shenandoah Valley. There are excellent markets down in the valley and roadside stands that offer great stuff like stone ground flour, honey, raw sugar, rolled oats, packaged trail mix, homemade granola, and all kinds of dried fruits, nuts, and canned home-grown vegetables.

I started a vegetable garden during the spring, and it has been quite successful. Working in the dirt runs in my family; my parents grew up on farms. Spending the first six years of life on the farm with my grandparents must have tied me to the land as well. This may be where my preference for fresh and natural foods originated. And, which was probably why, while picking berries, my mind kept wandering back to my beautiful confused guest asleep in the cabin.

The memory of her soft sweet voice saying good night still lingered in my mind. The sound reminded me of how long it's been since a woman bade me goodnight so tenderly. Even more aberrant was how long it's been since I'd allowed myself to think such thoughts. Doreen was like a door, crushing my playing hand or losing my voice, when singing was all I wanted to do. It never allows physical healing or psychological wholeness, so I coddled my heart with protective thoughts. The emptiness Doreen left behind caused me to close myself off from any female attachments to nurse my gashed heart. I never wanted to experience such pain and loss ever again. The hurt was so deep I gave my gashed heart plenty of time to heal. But, rather than healing, it simply scabbed over, creating a tough outer shell.

Now, this stranger's presence, with her beautiful eyes, curvaceous poses and soft voice, has picked that scab and revealed a festering sore oozing with repressed desires. Holding so tightly to memories of Doreen for so long, my grip became weak. Holding on as I did exhausted my grip. Now that she's entered my life, I'm unable to hold back my desire as those repressed feelings push their way to the surface once again. My resistance collapsed immediately under the pressure of her charm.

She's awakened cravings for pleasures only a woman can satisfy. Real Black men not only love black women, but they also cherish them. There's a craving to have one in your life. They add so much to one's existence, not just sexual pleasure or physical support, but inspiration. For black men because of social repression left over from slavery, being lynched for only looking at white women, black men are so unsure of their masculinity. Real black women are the only ones who truly understand this. And, when they do, they add an enriching quality that magnifies a Black man's ego. They enable us to rise above our mundane circumstances. Parson calls it *the transformational power of love.* A Black woman becomes part of your being, changing you from the inside out. It was that way with Doreen. And, having known the effect of such feminine energy, I recognized it happening all over again with this no-named stranger.

Encountering her made me hunger to taste sweet lips and feel gentle touches. Now such thoughts terrify me. I may not be able to control my pent-up passions now that she'd picked the lock and opened the cage door. *Can I trust myself alone with her, or will I succumb to such an enticing temptation to satisfy my lustful longings? Memories of her nude body, soft silky skin, and luscious breasts had me ravenous. Unknowingly, she opened the cage door: and now, is there nothing to hold back the beast within?*

I returned to the cabin, washed the berries, and was getting breakfast when I heard her melodiously sweet voice, which sounded like birds singing at sunrise.

"Good morning Jericho," came from the direction of her bed.

I turned and was greeted by a big broad smile. I replied, *"Good morning. How's the head?"* I noticed that while the knot had gone down, it left a purplish mark on her deep chocolate skin just above her left eye. *"I tried to keep cold compresses on it that first night, but you tossed and turned, so, well, you see. If you want, I will make another. Some people say raw steak is good to use, but as you know, around here, veggies rule."*

"No, that's alright. After not having anything on it yesterday, I'll just tough it out." She smiled while adding a bit of humor.

"Another great smile to start the day. Seeing a woman smile early in the morning pales the sunrise,

even with a bump. Do you have any idea how you got it or even out here in these mountains?"

"No." She replied without thinking about the question.

"This is all so strange. There is no way you walked in here in those dress shoes. Not only would they be ruined, but your feet would also be a mess. They don't look as though you walked very far on the pavement, there are no blisters. I was reminded how easily they form after getting you here."

"What do you mean, Jericho? How did you get me here since I have no idea where I was when you found me?"

Standing up quickly, she said, "Hold that thought. I'll be back shortly. Then you can tell me all about it." She disappeared into the bathroom.

She emerged, after about twenty minutes, looking refreshed. I got her a bowl and a spoon. She filled it with berries and granola and poured rice milk on it.

"Okay, how did you get me here?" She seemed

excited to learn more about her presence in a place she had no idea how she arrived. She asked as she finished preparing her cereal. "More importantly, why did you bother at all? My feelings about people are that they are mostly concerned about 'What's in it for me?' They're greedy, selfish, and power-hungry. A good job, a paycheck, and being comfortable are all most are concerned about. As far as extending a helping hand to anyone, 'Let the next man get his the way I got mine!' They are not about being 'thy brother's keeper.'"

For a girl with no memory, she seemed to have some pretty strong opinions on this subject. Unlike other times, there wasn't any forethought. She just came right out with it without any prompting. Her comments seemed to reflect deeply held beliefs. I thought about probing the subject but feared she would only shut down or tense up. The morning was going pretty well. So, I let the conversation flow.

"That was probably true for me for a large part of my life. Yes, that's probably how I felt too, but tragedy has a way of changing one's perspective. You're going along,

life's great, and all of a sudden, the bottom falls out of

everything. All the reasons you had for doing the things you were doing are gone. Under those circumstances, one can come to feel life is no longer worth living.

So, you let yourself go to hell. You stop caring about anything. Then, somehow, maybe God or some other benevolent spirit intervenes, and just as quickly, your life turns around. Somehow, life has meaning again. When something like that happens to you, you have to start looking at yourself and others as 'works in progress.' When your life follows such a scenario, that helpless person lying there could be you or someone you love or loved you at one time. That being the case, wouldn't you want someone to help them?"

"Yes, I hope I'd feel that way, but now I don't know anything about myself. I'm so confused. It's all like being down in a deep hole, calling for help, and all I get back is my echo. What can you believe about anything under such circumstances? How can you trust anything or anyone? Where do you go for answers? How do you know what you're experiencing or feeling is real? Is it safe to depend on anything? My life is a maze of questions. I feel I'm trapped in a shifting reality."

"I don't know if I thought about those things that way, but you asked earlier, and the thought of carrying you to the hospital did occur to me. But I learned some time ago not to trust doctors to always do the right thing. You never know what their real motives are. Sometimes, they have agendas, and then they turn people into human guinea pigs. Under such evil care, perfectly healthy and beautiful women like yourself are destroyed in hospitals."

She looked up from the bowl of cereal, I thought, perhaps to gauge my facial reaction. But then she asked,

"You think so? That I'm beautiful, that is?"

Her first question was a nonsequitur; it caught me by surprise. I expected her question to be related to hospitals destroying people rather than concerned about her attractiveness. She hadn't seemed a vain person. So I admitted, "Oh yes! Certainly, you're beautiful." Could she be just putting me on for conversation's sake, being the jester once again? She continued,

"I've thought of myself as pretty, maybe, but never beautiful. Don't you think my skin is too dark? The way things are in this society, I've always felt men preferred lighter-skinned women."

Even with amnesia, her question had some real basis. This statement seemed to be another deeply held conviction that she expressed without reservation. It may have been a revelation for her now rather than a confession to me. Surprisingly, my response popped out before I knew it, as though something compelled me to counter her negative thoughts about herself. "Don't be silly! Your rich dark complexion is your most attractive feature. When I saw you lying there, your skin with that silky sheen almost glowing, I wanted to."

"I know," she interrupted, "wipe some of the oil off my face!" She cut in, preventing my thoughts from betraying me. "My face does get shiny, but I don't like using a lot of makeup."

Her shiny face comments saved me from letting something slip that I didn't want her to know. I had visualized her lying in the steam chamber, not on the trail as she supposed. Her impromptu supposition told me a little more about her while bringing me back to where this conversation began. "Now we know you're suffering from a memory problem. Had I taken you to a hospital not knowing your name, I would have encountered problems. Unable to provide insurance or employment information, no identification, money, or contact information, as well as only a perfect stranger to check on you, you would have been at their mercy. In such a situation, they probably wouldn't have given me anything information after I delivered you. You probably would have ended up in a mental ward in some state institution. A beautiful girl like you would have been prey to some real fiends in such a place. You may never have come to your senses or found yourself again."

I could see my comments had painted a different picture of her situation in her mind. I noticed a dark foreboding reflected in her eyes as she quickly turned away from me. It was as if she feared her expression showed something she didn't want me to see. She wrapped her arms around herself; holding the opposite arm with the opposite hand, she leaned forward half bent over. She made a shuttering sound with her mouth, stood up suddenly, and walked hastily into the bathroom.

Her reaction to my words caught me by surprise. After about fifteen minutes, she came out slowly. I didn't know what to expect when she sat down again. I could see she'd washed her face once more. I believe she hoped to hide she'd been crying, but their telltale redness couldn't be hidden. Even though she'd boohooed in front of me before, those tears had something about them that made them very private and far too revealing. Perhaps, a realization accompanied them that made that took her some place her memory loss refused to allow her to go, especially in the presence of a perfect stranger.

I tried to make it appear as though I hadn't noticed her change in demeanor while taking our conversation in another direction. I hadn't meant to terrorize her with the grimness of her present predicament because the truth of it was quite sobering. It may have pricked her subconscious in a way one couldn't imagined. Watching her compose herself, I admitted that those considerations did not motivate my behavior. Looking back, I'm unsure what drove me to do what I did.

"So, you wanted to know how I got you here, and since you have no recollection, I will begin at the point

right before you passed out unconscious and I laid you on the ground. Observing you from my favorite stop along my jogging path across the meadow, from that distance for a while, I could not figure out what you were looking for so intently.

Then your attire was so odd, dressed as you were, I couldn't believe you were alone in the woods. As I told you after you woke up here, I thought you had gotten separated from your site seeing party. Once I walked up and asked what you were doing, you fainted. Laying on the ground unconscious, I had no way of knowing if you were dying or what. Nothing I did revived you. My dilemma was: Do I leave you there or bring you home with me? I was concerned if you were with someone and they arrived as you were being carried off unconscious, I'd have lots of explaining to do to the police. I checked your vital signs. If you were dying, and I was the only witness, I could have been in deep shit, trying to explain what happened.

Once I decided to bring you here, being a woman, I thought: I'll just carry her. Soon, I realized you weren't a bag of groceries I could carry in my arms or a sack I could fling over my shoulder. The trip from there to here is a little over a mile up three slopes covered with trees, bushes, thickets, and vines. There are stumps and drainage ditches. A stretcher was the only solution. But, I had only my clothes, as material for constructing a litter. So the only solution was to strip down to my underpants, t-shirt, and shoes."

"What?" She could not hold back her laughter. *"Did you strip for me? Now that's a show I would have loved to see."*

Again, she went someplace with her comment, which I couldn't have foreseen, but her face reflected a curious or intriguing gaze rather than humor.

"Why didn't you just go for help?" She asked.

"Go where for help? You must not remember my description of where you are. This cabin is the big city, for about thirty miles around, and I was the only help that may have happened by in days."

Your clothes weren't strong enough, and what would I have said if someone happened upon me while dragging an unconscious nude woman through the woods? How would I have explained?" Again, she found humor in my explanation. *"So, stripping down to my shorts, t-shirt, and shoes, and my half-nude body would probably seem heroic, definitely easier to explain.*

You can't imagine how difficult it was pulling you on that litter. My knees started to bleed from slipping down, and the poles I used to construct the litter were not smooth, so blisters formed on my hands, and berry vines gashed my legs. I couldn't do anything about my legs, so I ripped my t-shirt apart and wrapped my hands in it. Lugging you with both hands, I probably looked like a walking steak to every gnat, mosquito, and fly in the area which treated me as dinner."

I could see she was trying hard not to laugh at my description. So, I snickered to relieve the pressure on her not to giggle. With that, she burst into laughter again. Struggling to control herself, she apologized profusely,

"Ha-ha-ha-ha, excuse me, Jericho. He-he-ho-ho, I'm so sorry, but I can't help it. Ha-ha-ha-he-he-ho-ho-ho."

"That's all right. Go ahead, laugh your head off!"

Laughing It had to be good for her, even though it was at my expense. It was the first time she'd had anything to laugh about. It felt good seeing she hadn't lost her sense of humor, even though it was at my expense. I continued my story,

"All the while, you lay there on the stretcher like a corpus. That is until a small stump caught the footrest of the litter and dumped you on the ground."

"What?" Again she was overcome with laughter.

"Once that big butt of yours hit the ground, you began rolling downhill uncontrollably." Her eyes bucked as she exclaimed.

"Oh my God!"

Now, it was my turn, so I kicked in with the old, "Ha-ha-ha-ho-ho-he-he!" Trying to spread a little of the humor around. "Chasing after your rolling body, I tripped. Tumbling head over heels, like a cartwheel, I rolled past you and back down the hill faster than you."

Again the laughter started. Looking astonished, she asked,

"Do you mean I rolled back down the hill, still unconscious?" She continued laughing.

"Yes, you were still unconscious, but you rolled only about thirty or forty feet to the bottom of the second slope, where you landed on top of me."

"On top of you?" She howled after her question.

"Yes! It had to look like we were doing a 69 because your legs landed straddle my face, with my eyes staring at your butt."

With that, she roared even louder and harder with laughter! I thought the 69-quip would keep her spirit light regarding the tumble. Once her laughter slowly died, she asked,

"Jericho, what made you do it? Why did you go through all that pain and trouble for me, a woman you didn't know? No one would have known had you left me there. I was unconscious; I wouldn't have known."

My thoughts about Doreen created a chain reaction. "You're right." Then, like flashes of lightning exploding that rainy night with Killibrew, that image lit up my mind as I responded. "But, I would've known. Just think about it. If I'd left you there and you woke up in the middle of the night, out in the woods, alone in the dark, without any idea where you were or how you got there, you would have been terrified. I'm not sure your confused mind could have handled the shock. I didn't think about all of that, but now that I have, I'm even happier that I didn't leave you."

The humor was gone. A spaced-out look covered her face again. With her eyes popped wide and mouth hanging open, she snapped it shut before her response, "Yeah! Yeah! Me too!" My statement seemed like another wake-up call.

"Still Jericho, you put yourself through all that pain and suffering for me, a total stranger. Your hands, legs, and the bites on your body, may I see your hands?"

I showed them palms up. She took them in her hands one at a time and rubbed over them, carefully feeling each scar. "You know, I can't be sure, but I feel no man has ever endured anything like that for me. You were not going to tell me about any of that had I not asked, were you?"

"No, I wasn't. I didn't want you thinking about anything you were unaware of when it happened. Like now, I get the feeling you've started to see me differently, with some sense of obligation. But that wasn't my intention. What more can I say? You were a helpless woman, alone out there, not someone looking for a favor. What is done is done. That was yesterday. Today, you still have some real problems to address, not that stuff and feeling all grateful...." My voice tailed off.

She was still holding my left hand, gently stroking the palm. Her big bright eyes were looking kind of dreamy. You know that puppy dog stare, as she looked into my eyes. I sensed her gratitude growing every time she stroked my hand; the look in her eyes said, I need to do something to show my appreciation. I could see where this was going.

"Oh, look at the time!" I shouted suddenly. Panicking at the thought of her showing gratitude may lead to me screwing someone not quite right or in her right mind, like a 'handicapped' girl. Jumping up from the table as I said, "We've been sitting here talking all morning! It's past lunchtime. I haven't accomplished anything! You should be resting! You've had a pretty hard time! We've got to develop a plan to help you, and I need to take care of some things that were on my agenda before you dropped out of the sky into my life!" Talking fast and stepping backward, I struggled as I moved towards the door, trying to resist her tempting allure. I was being drawn to her by what seemed seductive strokes in my hands. At the same time, looking into her alluring eyes. I blurted abruptly "I need to chop some wood! I could be attending to my garden!" I continued throwing out excuses as I backpedaled. "Things are going undone around here while I sit here talking to you!" Turning quickly and heading for the door, I continued, "So, get some rest. I have work to do!"

A puzzled expression covered her face. I could allow that to stop my desperate escape attempt. Looking away quickly, I turned before she saw my eyes.

"Well, all right, Jericho!" She said,. "If you insist. I'll do as you say and try to rest."

Walking quickly out the door, I dared not to look at her, my panicky response was hope or prayer that she wouldn't say anything or touch me as I left. It was as if I felt her eyes on my back, pulling me back to her, as I went through the door. Escaping, I knew I couldn't allow myself to look back and see her lovely face for fear it would hold such a tempting invitation. I may have felt powerless to her magnetic pull. Unable to resist her seductive allure would have unleashed the beast within. The sound of the door slamming behind me was like a judicial reprieve, sparing me a fate I knew I would regret. Under the circumstances, I felt she would have submitted to my desire, but her willingness would have been out of thoughts of obligation and vulnerability. That was not what I desired from her. I felt she deserved better, and so did I!

Chapter VIII:

T.H.I.N.C

Relieved, as I escaped what I knew would have repulsed me after it was over. Those last moments revealed the dilemma she posed. More importantly, I have no idea how to handle it or *what to do*. With the two of us here alone, what is a man supposed to do after a polite conversation? Alone here, before she arrived, I had no problems like the ones she poses. Although protecting Archangel doesn't require much in the way of duties—checking the security system, maintaining the fences, and being ever vigilant—they kept me busy, so I didn't get bored.

On the other hand, I can't take her any place with me on the run, not knowing her identity. It would relieve some pressure if I could get off this rock, but I can't leave her alone. So, I'm stuck trying to resist her magnetism, which draws me or causes my testosterone to surge like big waves against a small boat. Then again, what should I make of her behavior? Is it her, or am I driving these impulses which threaten to push me over the edge? My dilemma continued to grow exponentially.

So very strange. I'd never experienced such surges of testosterone pulling on my masculine drives. I suppose it never had the opportunity to build up as it has over years since Dorrean has been gone. When the urge for sex became a conscious desire, I went out and satisfied it, like most hip-hoppers. Delaying gratification had no relevance. Women were too available to deny me their pleasure. They were everywhere. All I needed to do was pick one.

This girl's presence has upset everything. Mulling over these prospects, I considered the situation from a different perspective while walking toward the woodshed. If she's a government agent, it is already too late to run. If she has been sent in by those devils at Unidyn, they're after Jordan's network, which I must protect at all costs. Either way, the game may already be lost even though they haven't discovered Archangel because Lucifer's beautiful enchantress had beguiled me. Plunging headlong into rescuing her, I may have opened the door to Archangel and allowed in the very force I swore to protect it against. My good intentions, if they were, may have put everything in jeopardy.

Considering the situation, I did a turnabout. If she has suffered memory loss, my wanton desire to make love to a woman, whose not quite right in the head makes me feel like a rapist. Her bewitching presence has me craving the feel of her soft skin against mine. Such desires threatened to take control of me. Possessed by longing, I haven't felt in years, yet restrained by her condition, but trying to do what's right, is a madding dilemma. It boils down to the possibility that she might be Lucifer's temptress without even knowing it. If so, she is angling to draw me into doing Lucifer's bidding. Therefore, we both are doomed.

Picking up the ax, preparing to chop a block of wood, I saw no way out of this predicament. Suddenly, a thought flashed in my mind from my childhood. While watching nature documentaries as a youngster, I always wondered: *Why, bulls fought for mating rights when there were so many cows?* It's only now I can make the connection between physical activities and built-up testosterone. Fighting during mating rituals is not just about the right to mount females; it plays a role in clarifying the strongest gene pools for cows.

The dominant bull's job is to exhaust the loser's built-up testosterone, not kill him. Even though the challenger does not defeat the dominant bull, the fight can prove his genes are strong and, therefore, worthy of mating. If the younger challenger is weak, he will exhaust his testosterone quickly, reducing the possibility that he will have enough strength to mount young, immature, or physically weak females.

Maddeningly chopping cords of firewood, I exhausted myself. For about an hour, grunting and groaning, trying unsuccessfully to drown thoughts of her with sweat, I felt like a young bull desperate for sex. Then, over the sound of the ax against the wood and my grunts, I heard her soft melodic voice.

"Jericho! JERICHOOO!!!" Stopping, I turned and looked in the direction of that sweet sound. She held up a goblet. *"Want a cool drink of water? Come on in; I fixed lunch. You've got to be hungry,"* she called to me.

I sighed! There she stood on the porch with water in one hand and waving a towel with the other. I laid down the ax and walked up to the porch, where she waited. She passed the goblet. Taking it, I gulped a big refreshing drink. Feeling the cool liquid flow down my parched throat, it felt like a balmy breeze on a scorching day. Surprisingly, while swallowing, I felt the soft, gentle stroke of the towel on my back, almost too gentle to notice, definitely too soft to startle. Catering to my thirst, I hadn't noticed her quick move around behind me until the first soothing glide of the towel.

Now, for some reason, I felt as if I was lying on the bench in the steam chamber as she gently brought the towel over my shoulders and down my spine. Feeling exposed, I turned quickly and reached for the towel, but she moved it up to my face even quicker. It was as though she'd anticipated my move. But how could she have known what my reaction would be? So, resisting her natural comforting gestures would've been rude.

"My goodness Jericho," she said impulsively. *"You've worked up a sweat. You're dripping with preparation,*

like a faucet. Maybe I needed to help? All that chopping couldn't have helped those blisters on your hands. What do you think?"

Her questions pricked my mind with images of her nude body on the steam room table that had tormented me and driven me to the wood pile in the first place. I wondered if I'd told her what I was thinking, what would she have done? Instead, I said, *"It's a man thing."*

She continued wiping sweat from my neck and chest as she talked, looking up quickly, catching my eyes momentarily, then back down at the place she was wiping. Her care felt like grooming after a ritual mating battle.

"I found Tofurky and other fixings in the fridge to make deli sandwiches. I heated the last of your delicious soup too. I even made lemonade, my favorite drink. I hope that was alright?"

"Certainly," I quickly replied as we walked inside. So naturally, she played the perfect housewife, I thought. Was this a glimpse into her former life? Taking the towel from her hand, I went into the bathroom to clean up.

Her last comments about her lunch menu provided some interesting insight. She not only recognized Tofurky as a particular product, she remembered the context.

Application is one of the most sophisticated activities of the brain. No matter how simple the task or activity one undertakes, it requires the same short and long-term mental processes. This indicated her brain was functioning properly. Tofurky is a relatively new product for vegetarians, available only in a few markets. She also knew it was for sandwiches, which makes her knowledge very specific. Her recall was just as precise, remembering her love for lemonade, her favorite beverage. With her brain functioning normally, the prospect of her being a spy or agent added a greater sense of urgency to my efforts to figure out *what to do*.

Her memory problem wasn't related to damage or lost memories; it was probably due to interference from some defense mechanism, I presumed. Amnesia is just such a defense mechanism. It can kick in during stressful situations or sensory overload to block or interfere with the recall of certain events. I needed a strategy that enabled me to engage her mind's analytical and reflective processes in ways that had nothing to do with remembering her identity. If that worked, it may circumvent the defense mechanism and allow her to recall her past life.

This seemed my best chance of finding out if she was faking, even if I didn't discover her identity. While eating lunch, I would try my theory. Leaving the bathroom, I went to the living area and put in a CD, the *Best of Wes Montgomery*; his soft but upbeat music would provide a relaxing backdrop. *Wes* was strumming *A Day in the Life* as we settled down for lunch. I began, "So, you like lemonade, too?"

"Oh yes, there is nothing better than a cold glass of too-sweet lemonade and popcorn while reading, working at the computer, watching TV or a movie at night."

"What do you like to read?" I took advantage of the first opening to probe.

"Romance novels, biographies, history, short stories, you name it, I like them all.

I like reading, and it doesn't matter." She confessed freely.

"What about poetry? Do you like poetry? Even though I read other stuff, that's my favorite!"

"Yes, I like it, but I don't read much of it. Somehow, it feels kind of old-fashioned—you know, Edgar Allen Poe-ish."

Her comments flowed so fluidly; it was as if she didn't even notice she was talking about herself. These statements reflected personal preferences, habits, and experiences. They had nothing to do with work or information that could be used to identify her. And for me, that became the key. This was another indication her brain was working properly. I presumed the game her defense mechanism was playing was to disguise her identity. Similar to a hunter's blind, which they hid behind to disguise the present. Her real personality could be hiding in that fashion. Unseen, other aspects of her personality and life can parade freely before the world.

This allows her to escape knowing what's really

behind her memory loss. Consciously refusing to look behind it reduced her anxiety. It's like people who like watching horror movies but close their eyes to avoid seeing the scary parts. So, they must depend on others to tell them what it was all about. In other words, information related to her identity increased her stress level, which triggered the defense mechanism. I needed to keep her train of thought going but with some means of moving the focus away from her so her thoughts wouldn't cause tension.

During my inquiry, I needed to approach her from her bland side. So, I continued talking about reading to see where it leads. *"That's not the kind of poetry I read. I read Black poets and Harlem Renaissance writers. Have you read much of their works?"*

"NO, I don't think so. Who are you talking about?" She inquired.

"Writers such as Claude McKay, Zora Neale Hurston, Margaret Danner, Langston Hughes, Sterling Brown, Gwendolyn Brooks, and Walter Everett Hawkins, just to name a few. There are some great poets from Africa and the Caribbean, like

Christopher Okigbo, Derek Walcott, Alexis Wright, and Aime Césaire. Then, there are poets from the 1960s and 70s like Sonja Sanchez, Nikki Giovanni, and Maya Angelou. I'm reading a new hip-hop poet Yohannes Sharriff Smith. He has a book called T.H.I.N.C. (Teaching Humanity In New Consciousness: The Chrysalis of Evolution). Have you ever heard of him or his book?"

"No, but even if I had, I wouldn't remember it now."

There, that's exactly what I mean by the hunter's blind. Her memory loss seems to impose itself at particular times or in specific instances to explain not having a memory readily at hand, always to avoid certain topics. I didn't want her to feel pressured to remember, but the threat she represented to Archangel demanded I determine whether she had a memory loss or just some clever game going. This could very well be the end game for Archangel and me if I don't figure this out!

I needed something to pick at while trying to probe for information without making her feel under attack. *Go with what you know,* I thought. Misdirection could allow me to create a symbolic situation or setting that would dramatize her predicament's true nature but not demand her to think about who she is. A *"straw man"* could get inside her head and break through her mental block. If successful, it could shine a light on the psychological blindness her mind is hiding behind.

"After we finish lunch, I'll introduce you to Yohannes; he is a very interesting character. T.H.I.N.C. is about his first two years in college and his transformation, not only into a poet but a human being, as he puts it. Since you are a reader, I have a few other books you may want to take a look at. They're psychology books based on mind, memory, cognition, and learning."

"I've never read much psychology. Too much speculation for me."

"Speculation is good when you don't have any hard evidence to go on. That's exactly where we are with you and your identity problem—no hard evidence. That's why I want you to take a look at them; they may help you see that you haven't lost any of your memories. They are all still up there, and the problem is accessing them. That's not speculation."

"What are you saying? You think there's nothing wrong with me! That I'm faking?" She protested.

"No! No! That's not what I'm saying at all. Don't get tense and defensive!" I felt the conversation slipping away. The very thing I was trying to avoid was happening. Things were unraveling fast. I had to regain the initiative. I tried to soften my approach, *"The problem is some mechanism in your mind is preventing you from remembering, and that's normal in your condition. As I said, the mind protects itself from excess stress, sensory overload, and dissonant information with such mechanisms."*

"How do you know all of this? You could be just blowing smoke up my skit."

Now that was a thought I'd liked to have pursued. But instead, I said, *"You're right! However, psychology is a subject I've always been interested in, so I've done quite a lot of reading in that area."*

"So, I'm like a guinea pig for you, right." She seemed resistant to my prognosis.

<u>*"I wouldn't say that. Absent any hard evidence,*</u>

speculation is all we have. I'm

simply trying to approach your problem systematically. Psychological theory is about trying to understand behavior, not reading minds. It may seem complicated, but it's quite simple once you understand certain techniques.

Amnesia is one of the mind's defense mechanisms, but it's very poorly understood. For instance, there are several types. Take anterograde amnesia. That's when you have no memories of past experiences and events due to trauma. Catathymic amnesia is a complicated-sounding term, but it's simple, selective memory loss. Then one can lose their memory for a certain period, which is called Epochal amnesia. But, in your case, I think we're facing retrograde amnesia. This is the loss of memories for events and experiences directly after trauma, like a note in your head. It affects memories related to events just before the trauma.

"*How am I supposed to know which type I may have? It sounds like I may have them all at one time or another. Maybe that's why I can't remember anything about myself.*"

I didn't want to give a dissertation to explain amnesia. I hoped simply to help her understand her memory loss, and it didn't mean her brain had been damaged. I responded, *"That's the whole point of reading the books I spoke about. They will help you see you haven't lost your memories. Other than that small bump on your head, it doesn't appear you sustained any serious physical trauma that damaged your brain in a way that is preventing your brain from working properly."*

"I don't know, Jericho. If I haven't lost them, why can't I remember things like my name,"

She made that statement looking more confused than ever. *"Well, look at it like computer files that you've lost the codes or names for. The files are still in the computer, like your memories are still in your head; you just can't access them. Knowing why you can't remember will not bring your memory back, like knowing the files are in the computer won't allow you to get the information out without a code or password.*

These books, like computer manuals, may provide insight into your memory problems, which could help you understand your situation rationally. So you see, diagnosing your condition as amnesia only tells you possibly what, not why. That's the reason I want you to read them. I'll give them to you later. Right now, we are going to eat and enjoy lunch." I want to taste this wonderful looking sandwich! I backed off. The trick was to keep her subconscious from picking up on where I was headed before we got there.

The day passed quickly, and with the late lunch, the sun was already dipping behind the mountains when we settled down in the living area. I watched my beautiful befuddled-minded guest sprawled lazily on the rug in front of the fireplace. Her rumpled oversized outfit spoiled the scene for me. Besides, she didn't look comfortable. So, I said, *"Wait a minute, hold everything. This picture is all wrong. Lounging around the house in those baggy pants and that shirt just doesn't get it. I'll be right back. There are some things upstairs that will fit the situation better.*

I went into Jordan's upstairs closet and looked through his chest of drawers. I had seen women's lounging wear in there, nothing sexy, just comfortable.

Yes, here, this will do the trick. I went back downstairs and handed her the package. *"Here, try this on. The seal hasn't been broken on it either."*

"I don't know, Jericho. One of your women may get very upset when she returns, and someone has been wearing her things." She said, twisting up her face.

"Oh no, I don't have any women. Honestly, I'm kind of house-sitting here. The guy who owns the place is on the road a lot. He has all kinds of stuff around here, but I've never seen any women. So, go ahead and put it on. The package says medium. That looks about right. It may be a little tight around the breast and butt. You know you have quite a bite to put in it." I laughed following that quip.

"Oh, stop it, Jericho. You love making fun of my looks and shape."

She said with a slight smile as she headed for the bathroom. I was glad she didn't ask any questions about who I was house-sitting for. I would have had to come up with an answer that closed off questions really quickly. I didn't want to talk about that.

She rounded the stairs after coming back from the bathroom, and my eyes popped open as well as my mouth, at the sight of her. She looked like a different woman had suddenly appeared. I was right; she filled it out. It was floor length but was supposed to hang loosely from the shoulders over her body. However, her bountiful breast filled it out so completely that her nipples were visible. The gown was made of sheer silvery satin, and with every step, her hips swayed, causing the dress to shimmer with her gliding movements.

"Wow," jumped out of my mouth before I knew it."

"Don't you start Jericho," she said, wagging her finger. *"I know I don't look as good as the other women you guys have hanging around here, but this was your*

choice, not mine."

Her self-deprecating remark sounded almost apologetic. *"What do you mean? You look great! And, I told you, there aren't any women who hang around here. You shouldn't be so hard on yourself and your looks. I don't call you Miss Madison Avenue for nothing."*

"What? Who?" Now I know you are laughing on the inside. There isn't anything Madison Avenue about me." She continued disparaging her looks.

"I never said it to you, but when I saw you that first day, even from atop that hill, as far away as I was, you were a knockout. You're beautiful! I don't understand why you can't see that. Any man would jump at the chance to be with you. I know I would."

A blushing smile spread across her face as her eyes lit up.

"If you say so? You're probably only trying to keep my spirits up when you say things like that. I appreciate your efforts, Jericho. You're so nice to me." Her smile got even bigger with those words.

Already enthralled by her charm, I needed to change the subject. I reached out, took the books from the shelf, and said, *"Here are the books we talked about while we were eating."* I decided this would be a good time to bring Yohannes into our conversation as my *straw man*. He could draw attention away from my present thoughts of her while giving her something different to think about. Once more, I felt I was thinking like Killibrew when he introduced me to Yohannes on the ride after the raid on Unidyn.

"This is T.H.I.N.C, Yohannes' book; he was only twenty-two when he wrote it. What makes it interesting is he explores his mental state through narrative descriptions and poetry. It's a psychological exploration without a lot of theoretical explanations. He approaches life very intuitively. the poet in Yohannes believes that change is continuous, and one must embrace it as an essential aspect of growth.

According to Yohannes, it is the reaction to an experience that determines whether one progresses or retrogresses mentally. Either way, we are changed. The resulting change affects the individual in a particular way, and we emerge changed by the experience. Those who do not embrace change usually repress their thoughts. The fear of change initiates repressed behavioral patterns, which control their thoughts and actions, whether they realize it or not."

"Do you think I'm repressing my thoughts?" She asked.

"Well, there's a lot more to it than that, but I don't want to concentrate on you now. Let's concentrate on Yohannes and see what he has to say. This was Yohannes's thing. He felt trapped in existence not of his choosing. He saw himself as the little fat boy. And, because of that, he felt he was the brunt of jokes. But, once he left home and enrolled at Georgia Southern University, a small, predominantly white college, things changed for him. Not only was he someplace he'd never dreamed of being, but he also went from being in a majority-black environment to being in the minority. The important thing is nobody knew him. For the first time in his life, he began to experience the liberating power of choice. He was free of his past. No past meant he could be whomever he wished. He could make it up as he went along."

"How could he just stop being himself? That's who he was."

"Yohannes employed a kind of Catathymic or self-selected amnesia. He kept the character traits he desired and discarded those he despised. In other words, as much as possible, he consciously created a new personality, someone built based on his fantasies about the kind of person he thought he wanted to be."

"But wait, you can't just decide who you want to be and just be that person. How do you know who you will end up being?" She inquired.

"You don't. That's the point. The problem, as Yohannes discovered, is that even with a makeover, the new existence isn't without problems. There are consequences of life we must live out no matter who we are. Change one thing, something else changes, and we have to live with that reality. Some people call this the 'Butterfly effect.' Humans do not have erasers for wiping out those portions of life they don't like once they see the results. We can't go back or get a do-over to readjust things after the fact."

"Well, something surely erased my life; it's like I never lived to me."

"Yohannes learned, and I agree, we are all works in progress. We can't manage change like impartial observers. We are a part of the change, so we are changed by it. I found his book very educational; it taught me to see change as a metaphor for life. Here, take the books; you can read them later."

She talked about her life being erased, but she was clinging to the thought of a past life as though it could take the place of today. Clinging to the thought of having a past was like the reaction of someone abused or kidnapped; after a while, they form a strange attachment to their abuser or kidnapper. She might have been running away from that life, but feelings of guilt about her desire to escape may be causing her to verbalize acceptable and expected statements of real attachment to something she hated.

Chapter IX:

A Necessary Storm

Being lost, confused, or off the path isn't the worst thing. It happens to everyone at some point or another. The problem is not trying to find your way again or accepting where you are simply because you woke up there. Life is about the choices we make and how we respond to those circumstances in the most adaptive way that allows us to find the person we feel we were meant to be. This is all I was trying to help my confused guest do. She needed to get to where she started questioning herself about her life and wanted to know the real person that makes her.

So far, answering questions about her has been slow going. More importantly, why has she fought so hard to hold on to beliefs she thinks are the basis of her past life? I feel getting clarity about the situation, as it is now is the best place to find answers about the past. Although I was very empathetic towards this girl's condition when I encountered her, it was her threat potential to Archangel which drove me to investigate her presence in the mountain. However, her bewitching beauty has enthralled me, pulling me into her lost past. I'm trapped in the search for the truth of her, one way or the other.

The reality is if memory loss is the case, she believes her past is more important than her present. Even though I'm not sure how I must prompt a change in her psyche, she must become convinced that the present matters most because that is where she is. Her past is where she was and may not even exist now. Therefore, if she's going to live the life that is, it will be in the present because the past is already spent. It can't be changed.

For me, I can't be grasping at straws, so I'm going to use Yohannes. As a *strew man,* hopefully, he can help me bring her into the present in a way that doesn't require her to talk about herself. Probing for information about her has repeatedly triggered the mental defense that locks her mind up. Misdirection and subterfuge will be my guises to pick the lock and open the door to her past. So I began this way. *"Now, let's listen to Yohannes' poetry for a while. He's my favorite artist. Sunflower and Hands are two great cuts I like. You may like them also. Yohannes and I think alike, especially when it comes to women."*

"Oh! And, how is that Jericho?" That was the response I hoped for. She seemed intrigued.

"I'm not going to say; I want you to listen and see if you can pick up on it. If you do, you'll understand, and then there won't be a need to explain. If not, it'll give you something to think about instead of your problems. It's his hip-hop lyrics and poetic style that I like. Young hip-hoppers back then were very intuitive and quick-witted, very sensitive to love, family, and community. You may be that kind of person also."

"Well, I certainly hope so. I can't stand self-centered, greedy, money-grubbing people. They will destroy the world to make a dollar and get what they want."

She was lounging cat-like on the big Polar Bear rug when the CD began. I hoped to uncover new information that clarified whether she was an actual threat to

Archangel or just confused. My strategy was to make an end run around her psychologically blind. If successful, the CD would elude the defense, blocking her mind. The misdirection began with using Yohannes as the point of the conversation, which should allow focus of some not present, in time of fact. if she plays along she should relax and be reflective since her comments would be about someone she never met. If that happens, as she talks, she may give personal reflections that give insight into aspects of her life.

Without insight or background info into her personality, I'm hoping she will relate to Yohannes' message and identify with his hip-hop imagery, situations, and characters. This may prompt comments about her lifestyle—music she likes, places she goes, incidents she remembers, and so forth.

I didn't want her to see me as an observer, as she indicated with her guinea pig question. The CD was my blind to hide my strategy behind. Glancing at her quickly, then away as she lay, she changed positions from lying down to sitting up with her knees bent and her arms wrapped around them. Resting her head on her legs, she just listened. Interestingly, she began making comments like 'yeah,' 'you better know it,' 'that's right,' and 'right on my brother," emphasizing her agreement in response to Yohannes' hip-hop vibe.

When she looked up at me, I avoided her eyes, pretending to be so off into the poetry, so she wouldn't know I was observing her. Yet, from where I sat, she was on point with all the appropriate responses and in all the right places. So, I believed she was feeling it. When the seductive pieces began, her mood changed. She lay back on the rug again, looking at me with such alluring eyes, which I pretended not to see. They seemed to beckon me to join her, sprawling on the rug. She made slight movements and sensuous sounds, sometimes glancing up at me, flashing a smile. She exuded sensuality, which ignited my passion. The thought lingered in the back of my mind. If she had used her feminine wiles to beguile and bewitched me with all of her sexual teasing, which meant she was getting a better read on me than I was on her.

Her movements in that hot shimmering satin gown accentuated her voluptuous frame. I was fighting a losing battle, trying to pretend not to notice her. There was no hiding the way she excited me. It was becoming impossible not to think of sex, even though I thought of her as a handicapped girl. The fact that she gave just the kinds of indicators I hoped for, in the back of my mind, the questions continued lingering—Is she just playing me? When the CD ended, I was still wondering; what to do. How can I be sure? So, I waited for her response.

Smiling gleefully, she said, "Umm, yeah, I like that! Now, that's some poetry I will read and buy. I don't know what it was, but he made me feel something. Is that what you were talking about, Jericho?"

"Ah-h-h! Maybe." I was afraid to commit to such an open-ended question. Those thoughts in the back of my mind kept warning me about that. She seemed to know just what I wanted to see and hear. I wasn't quite sure what I would have been agreeing to now that I seemed to be as confused as she was about what was happening.

"I didn't know young Blacks were even interested in poetry, let alone doing it, especially like that. I thought young Blacks back then were only interested in gangster rap and thug lifestyles. This kind of poetry has certainly changed my mind. He is really good. Where is he from? Do you know?"

"Down South, Atlanta, all that's in his book."

"Where did you get his CD?"

"I ordered it online."

I felt confident my *straw man* game was working. I got a good personality read on her, but I was still unconvinced her memory loss was genuine. Yet, what could I do? Even if it was the fact remained she still could be out to destroy Archangel and me. Her amnesia, if it was real, didn't mean she wouldn't remember all of this later, especially if Unidyn was behind her.

The *straw man* game, if it got past her memory defenses, still couldn't guarantee the information read I got was valid. I had no choice but to play along and proceed as though her amnesia was a disguise. What I'd seen so far could have been characters that popped out of her head to fit the situation, so I still may not have gotten a real look at who was hiding behind that psychological blind. It seemed to me she didn't want to remember her past life or who she was. My confusion continued. I still couldn't trust her reactions as real indications of factual memory loss.

I began my probe this way, "You know your condition is not too different from how Yohannes approached his problem. But, in your case, your memory loss is involuntary."

"Why do you say that? He was just writing a book. What he says doesn't have to be real." She responded.

"Maybe not. It's all in how you look at it. What you aren't considering is just because something may or may not be true doesn't mean those realities aren't comparable to real-life situations. Your mind should help you determine what's real, not with it telling you what is real.

I believe Yohannes' point is that everyone has to make a life out of the existence they are born into, rather than just settling for the life they are given. In other words, everyone is born into a particular set of circumstances—their environment and inheritance—that's their frame of reference. "The fat boy was Yohannes' mental image of himself. It was an extension of his personality. Therefore he accepted it as a condition of life.

Most people develop a particular mindset about who they are, not who they can be. They accept their world as a reflection of who they are. Unknowingly, most of us never realize that's a choice we make. Similar to an umbilical cord, this subtle process feeds us perceptual clues about ourselves from our environment, which confirms who we are. Therefore, to act otherwise requires an internal realization or divine intervention for one to change."

"Do you think God is punishing me for Kimberly?" She said in a very matter-of-fact way.

"What did you say? Who is that? You said, Kimberly?" I asked quickly.

"What are you talking about?" She grimaced and tightened her eyes.

"You said, *"Do you think God is punishing me for Kimberly?"* I repeated quickly, trying to catch her defenses down.

"I did not!" Her face became even harder, with wrinkles.

"Yes, you said Kimberly!" I insisted.

"Well…, if I did, I have no idea why I would say such a thing. Who's Kimberly anyway?"

Now she seemed more relaxed, as though any memory of the entire incident had been swiped away. The moment I mentioned the name, Kimberly, I noticed she became very anxious. That was what I was afraid of; her mental defense reacted so quickly. It was as if she never had the thought, let alone expressed it. With her anxiety building, I took a detour. I didn't want her to tense up again.

"Well, anyway, one's identity is the past, and it's set; it is what happened. The future is what's going to be. The present is where things are done. That's where choice comes into play. Change begins in the present because that is where we are.

Choice means either one goes along with their existence, accepting it like their skin, or they break out of those confines like a butterfly frees itself from its chrysalis. You can choose to create a world that works for you. That is Yohannes' point. This is what I meant when I said your situation wasn't too different from his, and you weren't trying to remember your past."

"I don't know what else to do; I'm trying as hard as I can. Hmmm!" A forlorn sigh followed her declaration.

I jumped in quickly before her doldrums took control. *"Similarly, you are in the same place as Yohannes. He realized the kind of person he could be, and from that point forward, his life was a choice. That's all I'm saying about you and your circumstances. From this point forward, you have a choice. Think about it! Do you want to spend the rest of your life regretting a few could have been' when there are so many 'could be' waiting? Do you?"*

"But, I don't remember any of the dreams I had or who or what I wanted to be.

It's like I'm just here, going nowhere."

"What if you didn't spend all your time trying to remember who you were and start trying to live with the person you are? What would you do? I mean, just

start your life where you are now, not trying to think of yourself as bound by who you were. Yes, it is difficult to free oneself from their past. It is constantly acting on the present. The past can be a prison without walls because it exists in your head, not outside of you."

"I don't know, Jericho. That's easy for you to say. You aren't me! You don't have memory loss."

"What if you did as Yohannes? Just start making it up as you go along. Open yourself up to taking things as they are right now. What if you created a reality in your mind that this is the way things have always been and may always be? But, as things change, you are ready to change with them. What if you approached life as a work in progress? That will be a place to begin. Why do you have to remember your past to enjoy and love the person you are today? Maybe, if you weren't trying to remember,

everything would come back naturally.

Don't get me wrong! Remembering who you are is important. But, what I'm trying to point out is that the person you're trying so hard to remember may not be who you are. That person may be dominated by her fears, afraid to look the real you in the eyes. That person may very well be the one behind your memory loss. Maybe, it's she who is fighting to keep the real you locked up inside your head. Maybe you're caught up resisting the person you were and frightened by the prospect of being someone you have been running away from all your life. Knowing yourself will allow you to love yourself and receive God's most precious gift for human beings: love for self."

"Still, I don't know. You just met me. How can you be so sure about what my life was like? You are just saying things. How can I simply let go of my past? That's who I am."

"Those are your fears talking; they want you to hang on to what you've always believed. All your past does is give you something to base your fears on rather than something to hope for."

"But, you see, Jericho, you know who you are, why you're here, where you came from, and what life has in store for you."

"No! That's just it! What difference does any of that make here and now, in this place? Besides, nobody knows what tomorrow will bring. So, why try to anticipate it or worry about what's coming before it arrives? Sure, I know my history. I know who I am, but that doesn't guarantee anything."

"That all sounds so wishy-washy. How will I know what is proper? What's right? I need to know what to expect. I have to be able to count on something."

If this girl has amnesia, she is holding tightly to her beliefs. "Listen to yourself!" I admonished. "What can you count on now? Where is that something you can depend on at this very moment? You're reciting something that's in your head you've been told and accepted without questions. You talk like someone who is having a bad dream and know they're going to wake up and everything will be fine. I'm not wishing this on you, but what if this is what you have for the rest of your life? Then what?"

She had no response. Sitting on the rug looking wide-eyed, she resembled someone who expected this all to be over but was unsure whether she was asleep dreaming about being awake or awake wishing she was dreaming. She sat on the floor, wringing her hands while looking at them, not saying anything. After a few tense moments of silence, I went out onto the porch.

I walked about, breathing the cool crisp evening air. Stars had begun to appear in the heavens. Gazing upon them, I wondered: Why had the hand of fate moved so forcefully to bring such a beautiful enigma into my life? Shit! Why bother? Had what I did amount to anything good? Was she any closer to understanding herself? My head was spinning with thoughts of her when a voice I didn't want to hear sounded like a megaphone. It was Jordan mocking me.

Why do you even care? She doesn't mean anything to you. This is about saving Archangel. If she doesn't mean anything, why are you so restrained? Handicapped or loose in the head, it doesn't matter. It's your job to deal with the problem. No matter how beautiful it is and she is. She's still a threat to everybody involved with Archangel.

It's not just a matter of getting rid of her to relieve me of this haunting torment, I thought to myself. She has been here too long now for me to simply let her walk away. Without knowing one way or the other who she is, the threat to Archangel from Unidyn makes her leave a life or death consideration, even with erotic images dancing around in my head.

Glancing through the window, I could see her lounging on the rug without any idea what powerful images she conjured in my head. Urges that sent my erotic passions cascading wildly have created an insatiable longing to feel myself deep inside her. I could visualize us moving as one. Forget all of that; I should just take her where she lay! What to do?

So real were those almost overpowering desires to have her that first night. I could have climbed upon the steam table with her, but thoughts of Doreen restrained me. Flooded with repulsion because I considered taking advantage of someone so helpless and open to a violation, I was driven from the steam chamber. Chased by the same thoughts -- Who could blame a man under these circumstances? Who would know? Now I'm banished to the porch because I would know.

Know! Know what? It seemed I could still hear

Jordan prodding me. For all you know, she could have been a streetwalker back where she came from, ready and willing for any kind of sexual encounter at the right price. Maybe her coy facade is to cover up the fact that she's trash back in that world.

With those thoughts, visions of clubs and places I frequented in the past came to mind. The type of things such women did in those places, if your money was right, filled my head. Her face became superimposed over those images, which ignited my passion. Inwardly, a scintillating inferno blazed. Although the night air was cool, I began to perspire as urges spurred a throbbing that grew uncontrollably with each heartbeat. How could I repress it? I needed to do something to drive thoughts of her from my mind. I needed to get control of myself. *What to do?*

Snatching the front door open and stepping inside quickly. I saw her still sprawling on the rug, seductively inviting as she read. She turned the page with one hand and twirled a braid with the other. Rushing, I reached the staircase and turned, quickly avoiding her eyes. I was down the hallway before she saw me or did anything that may have drawn me to her in my out-of-control state of mind. Thankfully, I had eluded temptation once more. I grabbed the bathroom door handle. Rushing to get into the shower, I hastily reached for the doorknob, fumbling, I missing a good grip. Finally, as I entered the bathroom, I tore at my clothes. I stepped into the water, fully dressed.

I desperately needed to feel something cool against my skin. I had never had to restrain myself when the urge for sexual gratification was an issue. The frigid water poured over me, soothing my torrid body, but there is no shower for one's mind. Undressing after a while, the scene of a lake giving off its steamy mist on frosty mornings came to mind. I don't know how long I stood under the icy water before my body reacted to its frigid temperature. Even though I began to shiver, after a time, it was a relief from the burning emotions that were consuming me. However, that long cold drenching didn't purge me of the almost uncontrollable desire to possess my no-named guest fully and wildly, even in her mentally challenged state. The old bull didn't exhaust the young one fully; his need to mount remained.

I emerged from the bathroom and rounded the staircase. She still lay seductively stretched out on the rug; she glanced up at me. While her beautiful eyes flashed like lights, her face became adorned with an enchanting smile. Her enchanting eyes seemed to twinkle, flashing like lights; all of it came together and melted my frigid exterior. Hearing me as I rounded the stairs, she rolled over on her back. Resting on her elbows with her legs spread apart, and said, "Jericho is there anything I can do for you?" Her remark seemed more like an invitation than a question, and the temptation to accept was almost irresistible.

"There seemed to be something wrong when you entered the cabin. You entered so abruptly and stayed in the bathroom for so long. I was concerned."

Struggling to maintain the little composure that remained, I said, "No, there isn't anything wrong. Today was hard and long. I must have overdone it slightly while chopping wood. So I'm going to lay it down early."

"Yeah, I said that maybe I can give you a hot oil rub down and massage! I'm pretty good, you know!

Like a jack-in-the-box, she sprang up from reclining into a sitting position. Extending her hand and working her fingers to indicate her eagerness to please. Demonstrating her skills she said, "One always makes me feel better after a long hard day or a good workout, and you've had both. We don't have a proper bench, but that's all right. We can use the bed, or you can lie down right here," she said, patting the rug several times.

"No! No! That's all right! I will be fine after a good night's sleep." The thought of her hands rubbing softly across my body with my resistance already on "E" would have been more than I could stand. Thinking about the irony in her offer of a massage made me want to ask, *Where'd you learn to perform massages or how did she become so proficient,* but I didn't have the strength to pursue it.

"Well, alright. I'd be glad to do anything to make you feel better. Get some rest. I'll be right here if you change your mind. I think I'm going to read for a while longer. You were right, Yohannes is a very interesting writer, and I love his poetry. It's so down to earth. I think I may even go online for a while to see if there's anything new."

"If you want to get the latest on Yohannes while you're online, you can check out his web page on myspace.com."

"Ah yeah, okay. I might just do that."

"Cool!" I said as I slowly pulled myself up the stairs. "Remember, I'm just up here if you need anything. I am a very light sleeper, so give me a shout if you need anything. Good night!"

"Good night Jericho," she replied softly, then buried her head in *T.H.I.N.C* once

more.

Crawling into bed exhausted, her sweet voice was like a lullaby. Her voice

resembled an echo in a valley, reverberating in my head and returning like a melodic refrain. Why does her voice creep into my thoughts and linger in my head, like a song or a line from a poem, until I'm singing or reciting it? Then, there were her hypnotic eyes that bewitched me, pulling me into them, sucking me down into a whirlpool of desire. Those thoughts of desire and passion had rocked me to sleep every night since she came into my life, and this night was no exception.

I wasn't sure how long I laid there listening to her melodic voice and lines from *Sunflower*. Not quite sure whether I was dreaming or had simply dozed off, I thought I heard my name. Opening my eyes, a blinding flash of light lit up the cabin, followed immediately by a tremendous "BOOM" that exploded like the percussion of a bomb. It shook the cabin and I knew I'd been sound asleep. The reflection from another flash of lightning illuminated her head, peeping over the top step of the staircase.

"Jericho! Jericho!" She called frantically!

Another huge volley of lightning followed by thunder showed her fully up the stairs. The lightning's reflection off of her satin gown made it seem to glow in the dark. In rapid succession,as I answered her frantic call, a chorus of lightning and thunder drowned out my response.

"Jericho! Jericho!" She called once more.

I answered, while another burst of lightning and thunder filled the cabin, but revealed her standing near the foot of my bed pleading.

"Jericho, Jericho, are you asleep?"

Just as I answered, "No," another tremendous volley lit up and shook the cabin to its foundation it seemed, and she was in bed with me.

"May I stay up here with you for a while, just until the storm passes?"

She said, sliding closer and closer until she was right up under me. I could see she was terrified. She shook and flinched with each volley.

"Sure, you can." She finally heard me as she grabbed my arm, holding on to it with almost a death grip. *"I'm glad you came up. I'm afraid to be alone during storms too."*

Quickly she replied, *"Yeah, you are? Me too!!"* Hesitating, then she asked, *"What do you do when I'm not here?"*

Saying nothing, after a second or two, she nudged me with her elbow and said, *"You're just saying that to make me feel better, aren't you? I don't know why I'm so terrified."*

"Do you think you've always been this way?"

"I don't know. When the storm began, it was just rain, then the lightning and thunder began. It wasn't bad at first; the thunder was so far away. I turned off the computer and lights. I jumped into bed and pulled the blanket over my head. But then, it got worse, as the storm came nearer. I came up the stairs and sat near the top, but then it was like now, right over us. I could feel the cabin shake. With all the flashing and noise, I didn't know what else to do. You said you were a light sleeper and just holler if I ever needed you."

Still flinching and holding on to my arm as the assault of lightning and thunder continued outside, I tried to comfort her, "It's alright, just lie here. There isn't anything to worry about. The storm will pass, like everything else in life. Then, there will be clear skies and with a little cleaning up, it'll be like this never happened."

"I don't know why Jericho, especially since I woke up here just a couple of days ago, but you make me feel so safe and secure, protected. Do you know what I mean? I'm so comfortable around you; it's like I have known you all my life. When you explain things, it's like viola!" She said while snapping her fingers. "Its like I have nothing to worry about or fear. All I have to do is trust what you say. No matter the situation, somehow, things will be alright.

You know, it scares me that I have come to trust you so completely, so quickly when I don't even know you. Now, it's like, if you were not the person you are, what would I do? Jericho, it's frightening to think that without being in my right mind, I'm of no value to anyone, not even myself. Without any value, what good am I? Who wants a woman around that does not have any value for herself? What will I do when you grow tired of me around here? Where will I go? What will I do, Jericho?......... Jericho!!! Jericho, are you asleep? Well, I never. How can you sleep in all this noise?"

Pretending to have fallen asleep, I couldn't allow myself to answer. Perhaps, in my desire to help her, I had already made her feel too comfortable; it was like she had become a "straw woman." Similar to a butterfly, when someone peels its chrysalis away, what was thought of as help, actually makes the butterfly's wings weak and incapable of flight. For a butterfly, freeing itself from its chrysalis requires great struggle and internal will, which strengthen its wings for flight. Without struggling internally to know herself, even though she constantly talked about it, she may have lost the will to know the real person hiding between the psychological blind, hiding from herself.

Yes, I wanted her to stay here, but not at the expense of her never knowing who she is and choosing between that and me. That's the key; the loss of her memory was not synonymous with losing her mind. Pushed forward by the fast-moving events of these last few days, she's had to internalize a lot of new information—like the conversation we had earlier. She has been forced to make a lot of really difficult adjustments. Not knowing the real effect of any of this, my options are not clear.

The only thing I have to support the memory loss theory is Kimberly, who popped out once. But I don't have any idea who she is or what that means, even if she reappeared. If I'm right, her defense mechanism barred that door, and something drastic must happen for Kimberly to break through again. This whole thing has gotten very tricky. If I become too aggressive, her mind's defenses could shut her brain down completely.

Desperation and torment are a lethal combination when one's life hangs on a slender thread. I feared that the overpowering images, irresistible temptation, and maddening desire for her could push me over the edge. Driven to the edge, I looked over several times, but each time I pulled back. Concern for her mental condition and health didn't stop me. It was a voice inside I heard with my heart, not my ears. "You have a choice."

I know now, she's not an invalid because she can't remember her past. She understands the present, and that gives her a future. With that realization, I reconcile myself to the hand of fate. Her ability to make choices is intact, which means if she wants one, she can have a new life, but she has to make that choice. I will let the spirits guide me, whatever she decides.

More than beauty and hope in my life, in many

ways, this no-named stranger had already helped me let go of Doreen and start to deal with a hopeful future. Even though my desire to make love to her almost overwhelmed me at one time, I know now for certain it has to be her choice and not my urging. Thinking of her as I have been, I realized I had control of my actions. I could not have her as a prisoner of love; my actions must not determine her choice. Staying here with me must be an acknowledgment that she is choosing me because she has changed, and in changing, she wants me as I wanted her.

Chapter X:

The Perfect Storm (Beauty and The Beast)

Waking up the next morning, opening my eyes, I found her still curled up under me, fast asleep. Moving slowly so as not to wake her, I got out of bed; she was sleeping so peacefully. She needed every peaceful moment she could get. That scene triggered the memory of a song I loved when Doreen and I first met, *Wild Flower*. *New Birth* harmonized in my head as I went downstairs, after experiencing, what now, seemed like the perfect storm. Having been brought together in a way I had not imagined, her frightened spectacle had revealed a frightened child, not a devious plotting cunning and diva of Unudin. No agent worth their salt would allow a target to witness such a display of vulnerability, then sleep so peacefully, lying next to some they plan to kill or capture. No, that strom had brought us together that seemed to reveal two people struggle to find a place in life that offered new possibilities.

Only a few coals glowed in the fireplace, so I tossed in a big log, went into the kitchen, and put on a pot of coffee. I wanted to survey the storm's damage, so after my morning routine, I poured a cup and went outside.

Breathing in the cool, clear, clean, and crisp early morning air felt great. Nothing like in the city, no matter what happened, during the night, morning air remained stale with that dank sewer stench. Looking around, I discovered some tree damage—leaves and small branches lay scattered about—but none were down. All structures were intact, and erosion was minimal.

I walked about picking up debris. Faintly, like a far-off train whistle's lonesome wail, Jordan's voice pricked my mind. Unable to dismiss its presence or its force, his relentless reproof broke through, and I had to concede its power.

You are out on a limb now, and if you aren't very

careful, it will be like those you're picking up. Curled up with her all night! There's only one place this can go. She has her hook in you; I can tell!

She's afraid of storms. What are you talking about? I never laid a hand on her. Jordan, you're too suspicious. You make so much out of little things; Doreen was afraid of storms too. I pleaded.

That's what I mean. Deny as you may, Jericho, I know how these things work. You may want me to go away, just as I wish she would disappear, but neither will happen based on a wish.

I know Jordan. You've said it all before. Yes, her presence here endangers everything. I'm allowing this strange woman to jeopardize Archangel. Even if she's not an agent, she's acquiring knowledge that could be used to destroy us once she leaves.

I have to agree, she may not want to or plan to, but with their sophisticated deception, they'll disguise their intentions. So, she'll help them without knowing it. At this point, I'm not sure what to do with her. Could all my psychological talk have been my way of inviting her to stay and forget about the outside world? Am I seriously hoping she never remembers her former life, but even if she does, am I pollyannaishly wishing she'll stay on any way of her own free will, like 'Beauty and the Beast?' No, Jordan, there isn't any need to remind me that this little spark I'm playing with may explode into a forest fire and burn Archangel to the ground!"

Since you see your predicament so clearly, I'll say any more about what to do.

Sounds came from the cabin, and I looked towards the front door. It opened slowly as her head poked out.

"Oh, there you are. Aren't you cold out there so early in the morning? I can see my breath. Look!" She blew, and her breath condensed, looking like smoke in the crisp morning air. *"See! I know you have to be cold in only that sweater!"*

"No, I'm not. It's refreshing and exhilarating. You should come on outside and enjoy it for a while before breakfast."

"Hum-m-m-m! I don't have a coat."

"You're too much, the city girl. I bet you bundle up as soon as the temperature falls below fifty degrees," I said, walking toward the door.

"You got that right. We don't have any Eskimo blood in our family." We both chuckled a bit at her remark.

"I woke up and called you. When you didn't answer, I didn't know what to think. I never imagined waking up and you not being around when I opened my eyes. I know that's so silly of me, isn't it?"

"Not really," I responded as we walked inside. *"We had a rough night with the storm and all. I wanted to survey the damage. How are you this morning?"*

"Oh, I'm great! I slept like a baby. Is there much damage?"

"Nah! We've had much worse. Once we lost a whole row of trees along the outer edge on the Northside next to the cliff."

"Although one had nothing to do with the other after you took me into your bed, the storm passed quickly, or so it seemed. I thought you were awake. I was just

talking my fool head off while you were out like a light. How could you sleep with all that thunder exploding every two seconds? All that chopping wood seems to have worn you out. Maybe that's why Mr. Light Sleeper didn't hear me screaming at the top of my voice. What do you think?" She laughed.

"Listening to you talk about what mattered for the first time, I must have drifted off." With that remark, I wanted her to know I was listening, up to some point, rather than being so exhausted or playing possum to avoid answering her question. Looking at her luscious full lips, I wondered what she would do if I told her what I was actually thinking. Instead, I laid it off on trying to hear her soft voice over the sound of thunder in my ears rather than the powerful image she created in my mind.

"Sometimes, I overdo it, and then again, rain and storms are very relaxing to some people. I guess I'm one of them. For us, we realize storms are things we can't do anything about."

Trying to explain how I was able to sleep while trying to find a means of probing for more information, I thought about Killibrew's comments regarding feng shui and rain. *"Some people say storms are mysterious forces, an omen of things to come. They believe storms are a cleansing force, washing away the bad spirits from the past while clearing the way for the future."*

"That's interesting. You sure can get a lot out of a storm. They just frighten me. I don't remember anyone explaining it quite like that before. But, since I don't have a memory, there isn't any wonder."

"But you know, as I walked about cleaning up, I couldn't help but feel renewed, like some resolution had been reached. It was as if that was a perfect storm, which truly brought a new day. So, I must be one of those who believe storms are good things."

"You see, there you go again. That's what I was trying to tell you last night Jericho. You're always explaining things so well and making me feel everything is going to be just great. Listening to you, it's like my remembering who I am is just around the corner." She snapped her fingers in a 'voila!' gesture, as she did while talking during the storm last night.

"Maybe it is! You just have to believe that, and it'll

come. It's all up there," I said, pointing to my head. *"You keep working at it, and we'll get you out of here in a couple of days. I know you want to get back to wherever you came from, back to the people you love and those who love you."*

Although my feelings were going in the opposite direction, she needed to think I was doing everything possible to encourage her to remember, rather than wanting her to stay around. *"Did you find any leads online last night?"*

"Not a thing." She sounds dejected. Hoping to find a positive note to reverse her doldrums, I persisted.

"And you still don't remember any more names or anything else that may help us figure out who you are?"

"No."

"Well, do you remember anything about yourself before you woke up here?

"No"

"And you still don't know how you came to be in the mountains?

"No! No! No! There you go. Do you think I don't want to remember? Do you think I like your company so much that I would fake amnesia just to hang around here with you? Well? Do you?"

"Oh, no, that's not what I was implying. Hold on! Settle down! I'm on your side. I'm just trying to help you get a handle on this thing. Well, let's just have breakfast; I have cereal and fruit."

As we sat down and began eating, she remarked, "I know I've been here long enough, and you probably want to be rid of me."

Talking between bites, she continued, "Nobody wants to be stuck forever, taking care of someone about whom they know absolutely nothing." Swallowing, after sipping some juice, she resumed, "I'm willing to do whatever you want. You can take me wherever you wish."

"Why are you talking like that? Have I said anything to make you think I want to just get rid of you? I'm talking about helping you find out who you are. Even so, we may find your family. You have one.

You told me your mother's name is Ada; that's something to go on."

"But, you were grilling me. You sounded like you thought I wasn't trying to remember."

"I'm sorry if that's the way my questions made you feel. I didn't want you to come to think of yourself as a prisoner here because you can't remember your name, and I wasn't trying to help. Believe me. It isn't easy sleeping with a beautiful woman and having to restrain myself."

"Oh, Jericho! You're just saying that to make me feel better! We both know I'm not beautiful, and you have a better choice of women than me if you want it. The only reason you look at me twice is that you're stuck here taking care of me like a helpless invalid."

"That's not true! Why are you saying such things? I thought the storm passed over last night! If you feel that way about it, there is something we can do that may help."

"And, what's that, Jericho?" Her interrogative sounded depressingly sour.

"After breakfast, if you're up to it, we can walk back down the trail to where I found you. We can try to retrace your steps back in the direction it seemed you came. Maybe, we'll find something. Who knows, there may be people out there looking for you right now, a husband and family maybe. Yeah, a husband! He's probably crazy sick right now worrying about you; I would be."

Sitting at the breakfast bar across from me, she suddenly looked up from her food with a slight smile and asked, "You would...be worried sick, I mean?"

"Yes, certainly I would. Any man who wouldn't.... would need his head examined."

"Well, I'm not married, so I don't have a husband out there crazy sick looking, but I do have a daughter, her name is..."

Her voice trailed off, and her eyes tightened as "K-I-M-B-E-R-L-Y" rolled ever so slowly off of her tongue. This time, I didn't have to wonder about the impact of her statement on her.

"How do I know I have a daughter and her name and not remember my own? What's wrong with me? Am I crazy? What kind of mother am I? Where is my daughter now? If I don't have a husband, am I some kind of loose woman? Who's caring for her right this minute?"

There, Kimberly was the name she said yesterday but denied. Kimberly is her daughter. Up until that moment, she hadn't reacted to anything she said about her past. She had responded with almost indifference to her comments about it. Her anxiety level went through the roof on hearing a child's name a second earlier that she didn't even know she had. This was her first real reaction that had something to do with someone other than herself that caused fear or anxiety. Kimberly popping out, as she did, fractured her previously airtight defense. I wondered what else might come popping out if I kept her thinking about Kimberly.

Desperate for answers following the shock of having a daughter but not having any memory of her, tears began flowing. Considering the last time she got really upset and passed out, I moved quickly to preempt that. Going around the breakfast bar, I sat on a stool and pulled her close as she sobbed wildly. Not knowing anything about her, the right words to calm her didn't come easily. Gently hugging her, I stroked her head and rubbed her back. I fumbled, searching for comforting words.

"Ah, come on now, don't cry. We'll figure this thing out. We're not going to let it beat us. I don't know your name or what happened to you, but there is one thing I do know: you're not a loose woman. After being around you just a couple of days, I believe you are a wonderfully loving mother. I'm confident you wouldn't leave Kimberly unless she was in the best of care. I'm sure she loves you very much and can't wait until you return."

I continued holding her and lightly stroking her back. She clung tightly, wrapping her arms around my neck. Slowly, she stopped sobbing. Looking up from my shoulder with her tear-stained face so radiant, she asked,

"You think so, Jericho? Do you think that way about me? Do you think I'm a good mother? How can you be so sure? I'm not! Why can't I remember things? Why?"

Sensing her anxiety returning, I cut in, "That's why we're going to walk back down the trail. You may see something that jogs your memory. We may find something that belongs to you. I know you want to get back to Kimberly as soon as possible. Right? I've finished eating, have you?"

"Yes, I guess so!" She sounded unsure.

"So, let's go! However, your shoes and clothes are not made for the trail." I went to the chair beside the bed and picked up her camisole. Holding it up, I reminded her, "You were nearly eaten alive the last time you were out there wearing this top. And your mini-skirt can barely cover your ass. You would be lunch again out in the bush, and that snazzy satin gown is inside apparel. There are some more things around here I believe that are just about your size; let me look around."

After checking out Jordan's closet upstairs, I searched through his chest of drawers. There was women's attire that would have been more appropriate for her to wear than the stuff I gave her—those baggy pants and an oversize T-shirt—that first night I brought her here. Jordan must be a real party guy. Besides that snazzy gown, he had several women's outfits, complete with shoes, stockings, and panties. He even has lingerie.

Also, he must have liked women about this girl's size; everything seemed to be a close fit for her. I found a pair of boots, socks, pants, and tops. I grab some undergarments on the way back downstairs. I gave her the things. Okay, the paints and shirt still have tags on them, and the underwear are still in their package.

"Here, try these. There are a couple of pairs of socks; you may need more than one to fill the boots out. I believe they will do just fine if they are laced up well. On the other hand, you'll have no trouble filling these out. What do you think?"

I held up a pair of bright red spandex pants for her inspection. "Here," I said, handing them to her.

She looked at the shoes and the pants, then at me from the waist down to my feet. "The shoes look a little small for you, and the pants are certainly not your style.

They don't match your eyes," she snickered following her remark.

"It's a long story."

"I'm sure it is, but we got time."

"Get dressed so we can get on to something that matters." Being a woman, she belabored the point.

"Is this anything like that old saying, walk a mile in someone else's shoes before entertaining questions about the owner?"

"The bathroom is down there, or are you going to change right here?"

"You would love that, wouldn't you?"

"We got time."

"I thought you were in such a hurry?"

"Well, I've never been one to miss a good show."

"I bet you aren't." On that note, she sauntered off to the bathroom and closed the door behind her.

Running upstairs once more, thoughts of Kimberly played peek-a-boo in my head. A part of the puzzle now, I felt she gave me something to replace the straw man game. However, I had to use her presence in this dilemma very carefully; I didn't want to spook my very panicky guest, as I had earlier. Overstimulation could cause her mind to shut down completely and then what knowledge she had about how and why she ended up here would be locked in her head. Dressed for the hike, I went downstairs; she had already emerged from the bathroom dressed for the trail.

"Wow! And Wow! Again," exploded out of my mouth. I started fanning with my hand and pulling on my collard as though venting steam. "Wearing those, there's no way you can get lost in the woods. You make those pants look great! I hope we don't run into any old stags out there along the trail. Hell, if we do, I'll have a real fight on my hands. Maybe, I need to carry a gun to protect you."

"Stop it, Jericho! One would think you've not been with a woman in years. I've heard stories about mountain Daisy Mays with their pigtails, big boobs, and tight shorts. They probably make me look like an old shoe to you."

"Now, you're the one who needs to stop it. In those blazing red hot pants, you're *sizzling!* You'll probably set the mountain on fire. 'Da roof! Da roof! Da roof is on fire. They don't need no water; let the motherfucker burn!"

"Jericho, you're full of it!"

"Not like those pants. They're full of it, and it's all you."

"Jericho! Stop making fun of me! I know these pants probably belonged to some girl you picked up off the trail, just like you did me. A handsome guy like you has probably found one or two on your doorstep. Those girls in these pants, probably make them look like a sack on me."

She walked as she talked. I notice a twinkle or mischievous glow in her eyes. I believed she knew how great she looked to me. Her whole conversation was one big tease to entice me to react and say more about how great she looked.

With a t-shirt underneath, an overshirt pulled tight and tied in a knot, accentuating her petite waist and the full roundness of her hips and pear-shaped derriere, she had me burning up. My eyes were bulging out of my head. I had to use my hand to close my mouth. Walking and turning, acting as though she was unaware of that massive bulge sticking out behind, her strides were calculated.

Moving so fluidly, she paused and posed as though modeling on a runway; guys pay big bucks for such a show. Unable to look away as she strutted back and forth, giving me an eye full of her eye-popping rear, it's a wonder I didn't have to use my hand to push my eyes back into my head.

Once, while turning, it seemed, she made her butt do a little jiggle. I don't know. I couldn't be certain! One minute, I was sitting on a stool at the bar, leaning over to one side, trying to get a double take of her ass. Suddenly, my head seemed to weigh a ton, which meant I couldn't stop its momentum. My hand missed catching the corner of the bar as I tried to stop myself from falling. The next thing I knew, I was on the floor looking like the stool was riding me.

Switching around, shaking her butt, she looked back with a half-startled gaze and then let out a big laugh. I believe she thought I did it to entertain her.

"Ha-ha-ha-! Oh! Jericho! I am not impressed. Ha-ha-ha! Stop clowning around.

You are so silly! Ha-ha-ha-a-a-a-r-r-r!" She said between outbursts of laughter.

Struggling to get my legs and feet untangled from the stool and up off the floor, I joined in the laughter, the perfect rouge to hide my embarrassment.

While she continued to model her exquisite frame, it occurred to me that maybe what I was seeing wasn't examples of her past personality, but uninhibited characters popping out through cracks in her mental defense mechanism. She had a large repertoire if she read and watched movies as much as she indicated. Was this model I was observing a character escaping her mental prison? Disguised as such characters, her real personality could be peeping around the corner of her psychological blind snickering.

Parading, she reminded me of expressions guys in the hood used to describe massive derrieres—backfield in motion or the recitation; *It must be jelly, cause jam don't shake like that.* Her slight smile told me she was enjoying the lustful spellbound way my eyes were glued on those bright red pants covering her lower body.

Feeling perspiration beading all over and my heart racing wildly, I begged, *"If we're going to do this... we'd better get started now, before an excursion into something going on here takes up the rest of the day I, I believe the outfit you have on will do*

just fine!"

The laughing and modeling had turned her on. She seemed to blossom similar to flowers after a rain. I grabbed a knapsack, and we hit the trail.

Chapter XI:
A Deserted Landscape

Going outside of the cabin, her upbeat mood continued. As we left, going down the walk, she flashed a big smile and chatted about the beautiful day. I slowed down to fall behind her, to get a wide-angle view of her against nature's backdrop. I wanted to observe the fullness of her beautiful frame adorned in red spandex, bouncing up and down. Having seen her body nude, her clothes added a greater air of intrigue. Entranced by the dalliance of her derriere as she walked ahead, the train-like persistence of Jordan's voice forced its way back into my consciousness. Walking down the drive leading to the spot on the trail where this whole mystery began, it was as if Jordan was sitting on my shoulder.

"Let me get this straight! You've been taken in by all those tears? You haven't learned yet that women can blubber about anything at the drop of a hat. Man, you're in deep shit! And all that, what kind of mother am I or loose woman jazz was nothing but a crock. You seem to have lost sight of where you are and why I left you in charge of all of this. A lot is riding on you and whether or not you can take care of business, Jericho. If the truth about this place falls into the wrong hands, years of work and many souls will be lost. This isn't a walk in the park for the people involved in Archangel. But, if your head is in the right place, this is a great move. All you need to do is take her down the trail a good piece and just fade into the bushes as I taught you. If she finds her way back, then you'll know she's no babe in the woods. If she doesn't, well, the problem is solved."

"Come off of it Jordan," I thought. "Those boots and red spandex pants she's wearing didn't walk in here by themselves. Besides, there are a few other things around the cabin that belonged to women unless someone was cross-dressing. Previously, I lived my life like a kid playing with fire, never thinking about the implications of my actions or the impact on others, but now this stranger has awakened a concern for more than revenge in me. I don't know why or how her presence has made such a difference in such a short time, but some of the larger issues you've always talked about have taken on personal significance. So, just back off and let me handle this my way."

This was the first time she'd left the cabin since arriving unconscious, so she had no idea what its surroundings looked like, beyond her view from the porch or windows. Walking down the drive to where the trail began, she was fascinated by the scenery. Going on and on about the trees, birds, wildflowers, butterflies, squirrels, and chipmunks—her eyes sparkled. She was like a little kid on a nature walk or field trip, touching things, smelling flowers, and grabbing my arm as she pointed out different creatures.

The idea that she was an agent didn't fit this girl. Her genuine excitement as she interacted with the environment was that of someone not accustomed to being in the wilderness. After my sessions with Jordan, if she had been trained as an agent, being in the woods for her should be like it was for me. All of this should be something to be mindful of, not something to get excited about.

We came up on the path leading to the trail with the three tiers of slopes. "Here's where we leave the pavement. This is the easy part. You have to watch out for....."

"Oh! Look, Jericho! A rabbit! Isn't it sweet? A-a-ah-h-h-h!! It's such a darling!"

"I guess there isn't any need to warn you about small furry creatures jumping out and startling you, is there? We're coming up on the part of the trail I told you about. Looking down, it won't seem half as daunting as looking up, and knowing, you have about one hundred fifty or so pounds to drag up."

"I don't weigh that much Jericho. It's just that I have big bones."

"That's what I said. Anyone looking at you wouldn't guess a pound over one hundred." She looked at me and burst into laughter. She hit me on my arm softly as I raised it.

"Oh Jericho, you are so full of it! You love making fun

of me, don't you?"

"Who me? I'm just the guy walking by. You, on the other hand, slept on the trip all the way to the cabin, big bones and all."

"I wasn't asleep! I was unconscious! There is a difference, you know."

"Yeah! Whatever. You still weigh the same," I quipped. "That rain last night probably made going downhill a little tricky in places. Use the trees where you need to steady yourself. Here take this stick just in case there aren't any trees nearby. Avoid walking in the trenches, because they can be really soft in places; you may be in mud up to your knees before you know it. Use the stick to poke around to see if the ground is soft or firm."

It was like someone rang the dinner bell once we began descending the slope. Every gnat, fly, and mosquito for miles around zeroed in on us. Watching her swat at them and trying to keep her balance started to look like a strange ritual dance. So, I gave her the advice Jordan gave me about being in the woods. "All these creatures you encounter live here; you're walking through their living or dining room. You're the intruder; they're responding naturally to your presence. They aren't going away; you need to develop a tolerance level for their presence and don't let them bother you. Your clothes are your protection. Simply try to keep them out of your face, and you'll enjoy being in the woods."

"That's easy for you to say, Jericho! They've had your tough ass for dinner for months and have probably gotten tired of it. They want new meat like me; that's why you don't have to worry about them biting you alive. They are loving me to death."

"Okay, since you can't handle the insects here, rub some of these calamine leaves on your exposed skin. It will keep the mosquitoes, gnats, biting flies, and fleas away."

"I don't know Jericho? That's not poison ivy, is it? You're not trying to pull some kind of sick joke on me, like in the movie "Vacation" are you because I've never been in the woods before, are you?" She asked with a tight-eyed grimmest.

"Oh! plants like Calamine and Jasmine are the base for most insect repellents. You've heard of Jasmine, haven't you heard that before? People keep Jasmine as houseplants. It also grows in the wild. It's a great floral addition to a garden or home."

"What does it do?" my skin is very sensitive, She asked, still cautious.

"It's like citronella. You've heard of that, haven't you?"

"I'm from the city, not stupid Jericho." She said resentfully.

"Well, Calamine and Jasmine release their scent when touched. It works best when the leaves are crushed and rubbed on the skin. Mosquitoes and other insects are supposed to be offended and avoid their lemongrass smell.

"Oh alright, I'll try it. But if I swell up or grow big ugly bumps and welts, I'm going to kill you."

"Ha! Ha! Ha! Ha!!" I couldn't help laughing at her. So I said, "Here, let me help you." While crushing the leaves, I thought about her "never being in the woods before" comment. This statement was very curious. However, considering the way she was dressed makes it very believable. All of it contributed to my confusion about how and why she ended up wandering around on the trail alone, which is why the agent scenaro was so palatable.

"Well, look at it from these insects' point of view. If our situations were reversed and I had the choice of biting your ass or mine, I would be all over you too! We don't grow dumb ass creatures around here either." I countered her earlier joke about not having Eskimo blood.

"You're not a comedian Jericho. I never laugh at sick immature jokes." She said, wrinkling her nose and turning her head while closing her eyes; truly, a classic Black woman's response mimicked a fictional female character from a book or movie.

We reached the bottom of the last slope, still laughing heartily at one another's attempt at humor. Looking back towards the top of the slope, I knew her appreciation for what I endured getting her to the cabin would increase exponentially.

"Wow, Jericho! You drag me all the way up there? Listening to your description of it, I couldn't imagine this hill being so big. What made you do such a thing for someone you didn't know? Stripping down to only your boxers and shoes, with these damn mosquitoes and things biting you all over, man, that took something! I don't believe I've ever thanked you for all you endured saving me. Please forgive me for how I acted that first night Jericho. I was so thoughtless and selfish. I was concerned only for myself; you're truly a wonderful person."

"Oh well, you're welcome, and besides that all behind us, you were helpless. We have a full day in front of us, so let's get on with it. We don't need to waste time talking about the past. It's the future we'd better get on with."

I grabbed her by the arm and started walking down the trail, pulling her as she looked back over her shoulder at the slopes. I could see that look of gratitude on her face. The way she was caressing and rubbing on my arm was all about obligation and what can I do to show my appreciation. I didn't want any of that from her, so I pulled her down the trail with me, before she got too sentimental about it.

Approaching the meadow, I explained, "We'd better keep to the high edge near the trees, making our way around to the area where I saw you searching. This area is shaped like a bowl; it drains the surrounding hills. It has openings at each end. The meadow in the center collects and funnels rainwater along beside the trail as it runs off. You can see the storm left lots of small puddles standing in places across the meadow. This is the spot where I first saw you. You were searching there in that tall grass around those bushes." I pointed as I explained.

"Although I can't be sure, the way this area is built up, I think you came in through one of the open ends rather than down one of the slopes. I watched you from up there on that ridge." I pointed toward my favorite stop along my jogging path. "After about fifteen minutes or so, I came down to see what you were looking for so intently. Does any of this make any sense to you? Got any idea what you were looking for in the grass?"

"Not a clue. To be honest, I don't have any

recollection of ever being here."

"While you searched, you kept repeating, 'I know it's here somewhere, I know it's

here.' Got any idea what you were talking about?"

"Not the foggiest. None of this means anything to me."

"Let's look around here in the grass for a little while; we may find something. Be careful where you step. It may be something very small."

"How will I know what it is if I see it since I have no idea what we're looking

for?"

"All I can say is, whatever it is, it will be something you wouldn't expect to find

in the grass in the woods."

We searched around for about ten or fifteen minutes but found nothing. I kept listening, hoping she would lapse back into her searching state of mind and repeat those phrases she was mumbling, but she never did.

Finally, I called it quits.

"Knowing the area as I do, since your clothes weren't ripped and torn and your shoes didn't look as if you had been crawling through the underbrush, I think you came through that opening. Your clothes had mud on them, and the only place you could have gotten mud on you soft enough to dry in patches would be around Lake Shoshone. If you were camping, that is probably where you were. I think we should go in that direction."

"Okay, Bawanna." She laughed at her Tarzan joke.

I let it pass. I figured at the clip she was reeling them off. I'd have plenty of opportunities before this safari was over. Still all wide-eyed and amazed as we walked, she observed, "This is truly some beautiful country; it's hard to imagine having been here and not remembering any of it. There should be some recognition of something so placid and picturesque."

"If you were out camping, you may have gone off on your own, marveling at the scenery, like now, and gotten separated from your party. You could have gotten turned around and gone in the wrong direction, which is very easy to do, even in the city."

"Oh!! Look, Jericho, a deer!"

"Yeah, they are all over the place."

"I never saw real live deer before, you know, like out in the wild."

"Well, you know any live deer you see are wild. People don't keep them like cats, you know."

"You just made that up trying to get a laugh. Didn't you? I lost my memory, not my sense of humor, Jericho. But, even without memory, I told you, I don't laugh at sick jokes like that."

"Whatever, back to the matter at hand." We continued trying to tease out a possible scenario that explained her presence. "It's very slippery around here; you could very easily have fallen down an embankment, hit your head, knocked yourself unconscious, and lay there for hours. That would explain the knot on your forehead. You may have fallen into the lake, suffered hypothermia, and gone into shock. Plus, with the blow on the head, hours of exposure to the elements, wandering around wet, cold, tired, hungry, and suffering psychological trauma, your mind may have blocked the entire period out. Such events could have triggered a defense mechanism to prevent serious mental damage. That would help explain why you have no recollection of ever being here."

"I guess so, Jericho. It's obvious I've got to trust you on all this being lost in the woods and what may have happened. Other than going away to school, I hardly left the city, except on a couple of group climbing trips with Margie."

"What school was that?

"What? Oh, I don't remember." She didn't even try. Maybe school had some connection to work, the way she automatically blocked it out. So, I decided to let it pass.

"Could something like a group trip be the reason you were out here? If you were on an excursion, surely they have reported you missing by now. They may be out searching for you as we speak."

"I just don't know Jericho; none of this means anything to me."

We emerged from the trees with a full view of the lake shimmering in the noon sunlight. "This is Lake Shoshone. Do you have any memory of being around here? Could you've been fishing? Most people fish down around the hatchery about ten miles from here at Lake Moomaw-Gathright Dam. That is the big recreation area for tours and fishing junkets. It's a 2,600-acre lake stocked several times a year with trout large enough to catch and keep; it has a size limit of 16 inches, and the daily creel is two. Only those who consider themselves real anglers come up here. This lake is one of several smaller reservoirs created as spillways to prevent flooding, as well as drain off excess water from the Jackson River. It's not very big now, but if need be, all of this area can be flooded to protect the valley below."

I provided all that information to see if she responded to any of it. It's the kind of common stuff anglers are interested in when selecting a place to fish. Had she been part of a fishing party, she may have responded to some of it, like the stuff about school. We searched around the lake for about an hour to no avail.

"This place looks deserted to me, Jericho. It doesn't

appear anyone has camped here in weeks. If I'd been here with other people, even if they left breadcrumbs behind for me to follow, birds and squirrels have eaten all by now."

"So, you're not disappointed we haven't found anything to help shed a little light on your situation?"

"Well, of course I hoped we would, but that's like every moment of the day. Am I always hoping my memory will return the next second? Sure, but it never does. But am I disappointed that it doesn't? No, I just keep hoping."

"Now that's what I'm talking about, a good strong positive attitude. I packed sandwiches, muffins, and juice for lunch; let's eat."

We surveyed the shady area near the upper part of the lake close to the spillway for the best place to eat. *"Miles above here, the rushing waters of the Calfpasture, Cowpastur, and Bullpaster tributaries combine to form the Jackson River. It is great here on hot days. Water rushing down the spillway creating cataracts that release soft cooling mist as water pours into the lake."*

"You're right. It's nice here, like pictures in magazines, on tourist posters or calendars." she said musingly. Then she did a pirouette, extending her arms above her head as she spoke and twirled.

The place we found had a few boulders and a flat area with grass. It was like being on an outing in the park. We rested after eating. Not saying anything, we simply lay together and listened to the symphony of cascading water, songbirds, and the breeze rustling leaves in the trees. Lying on the soft grass with the gentle breeze blowing in off the lake, she dozed off before I knew it, so I let her sleep.

Chapter XII:

Life's Call the Awakening Heart to Kill

Watching her sleeping so peacefully, I found it difficult to believe she possessed any sinister intent. Thinking back, she hadn't sought any information about anything, nor had she seemed interested in the cabin or its general surroundings. If her memory loss wasn't genuine, she had given one hell of a performance up to this point. A secret agent would be a colossal waste of her time and talent. This girl should be in Hollywood, winning academy awards. She awoke, sat up suddenly, and looked around as though afraid she was alone.

"Jericho, Jericho!" She repeated quickly.

"I'm here." Stepping from behind the bush that concealed me, I didn't want her to awaken suddenly, as

she did, and catch me staring at her, like when she was eating. She let go, a similar soft sigh as the one she released when I returned from outside the first night after regaining consciousness. Her eyes brightened, in much the same manner, even without the shadows and flames from the fireplace.

"Have a good nap?" I inquired.

"Wheeeewww!" She stretched and yawned. *"I must have dozed off. It's so peaceful here. You shouldn't have let me sleep like that. How long was I out?"*

"Not long. It was a power nap. You needed the rest."

"Why? What do we do now, head back to the cabin?

"No, there's another camping area north of here. We probably won't find anything, but we should check it out. It's a little over five miles along the road but much less through the woods."

"Though the woods?" Smiling, she asked, *"Is this anything like taking the shortcut to grandma's house,* Mr. Wolf?"

She fluttered her eyelashes, batting her eyes quickly

several times while flashing a fake smile, with her hands clasped beneath her chin. This, had to be, *Pretty Penny* popping out, the character that charms *Dudley Dooright,* or was her personality so dynamic in her other life, she did such things?

"For a woman with no memory, you are certainly full of it today!" I gave a few chuckles to let her know I recognized the humor.

"This is a favorite area for bird watchers, wildflowers lovers, and other plant enthusiasts, as well as those who come to observe woodland creatures; you seemed to fit all those categories, leaving the cabin. Our walk to the other area will be another opportunity for you to enjoy nature's bounty."

"Okay, I've certainly enjoyed myself thus far."

So cooperative! I anticipated her willingness to continue the outdoor adventure. However, I didn't anticipate the difficulty the storm-drenched landscape would present. The farther up the trail we went, the more difficult the climb became. Headed towards an overlook atop a plateau, a favorite campsite for nature lovers, we were going almost straight up.

Starting on flat terrain, smaller hills led up to a narrow winding ridge with a rather steep slope. Along this stretch, medium-sized trees and bushes grew thickly, covering the trail almost entirely in places.

Beginning at the small hills, I helped her negotiate tight spots, holding back branches and steadying her when her feet slipped on the rain-soaked ground. We encountered several very slippery embankments, on the small hills; the steep grade caused her to slide backward, creating difficulty in maintaining her balance. Helping her, I pulled with one hand and caught her other while I lifted her upward.

During one such exchange, I missed her hand but managed to catch her around the waist before she fell. Holding her momentarily in that close embrace, I allowed her to slide to the ground slowly. This was the first time we were in this position with our bodies pressed firmly against one another, without some stressful event promoting it. I could feel the softness of her breasts against my chest. Clutching her and looking into her eyes, our bodies said something our mouths never had.

Slipping from my grasp, she turned quickly when her feet touched the ground as I released her hand. Saying nothing, we continued struggling with the rough terrain. The small slopes of slippery soil gave way to a narrow rocky ledge with a drop-off of a few hundred feet on one side and the sheer wall of the plateau on the other. Along this stretch, limbs from smaller trees and bushes encroached on the trail in a few places, reducing the path to only a couple of feet or so. Approaching these areas, I held back branches as she slid by. After looking into the abyss, she held on to me for safety, trying to avoid getting too close to the edge.

At one point in negotiating the bushes, we were face to face. Pelvis against pelvis as she slid by, I felt her breasts rub against my chest as she held on sliding by me. I looked down as she looked up. We were within kissing distance. Realizing our proximity, she pushed back slightly, glanced up then looked at the ground again. When the next clump of branches hanging over the trail appeared, we looked at each other and then away quickly.

This time squeezing passed she turned her back toward me. Facing forward to avoid the implications of being pelvis to pelvis again, she could see over the narrow ledge into the abyss. Pushing back against me, her butt pressed against my groin as it passed. The softness of her butt glided across my crotch, making the spandex flex to the contour of my pelvis. Her butt rubbed slowly against my groin sliding across, which felt like strokes, sliding by.

Squarely in front of me, the recess of her cheeks with her derrière squarely in the center felt like a caress to me, causing an instant erection. The cheeks of her butt felt like they were holding and gently caressing it. I knew she felt its hardened state because she jumped forward, almost losing her balance. Afraid of falling, she reached back around, grabbing my butt for balance. Her desperate move to save herself pulled me even tighter against her derrière. Pressing even tighter, she couldn't move for a long second or so. Stuck there for that long minute, I reached out and grabbed her around the chest to pull her back from the edge, but my hand clutched one of her luscious breasts. Feeling her hardened nipple against the palm of my hand and her soft butt caressing my erection, neither of us could move for a long moment. Still clasping her breast with one hand, trying to pull her back from the abyss, I clung to a branch with my other hand until we fell back against the cliff wall. We were locked together there in that embrace for what seemed like an eternity.

Consumed by the scent of her moist, soft perspiration-drenched braids against my face, the aroma was like a vacuum cleaner sucking my mind blank. Momentarily, inhaling her pheromones, which had such aromatic sweetness, I seemed to lose consciousness due to her fragrance. Pressed together, not moving, with the cheeks of her soft derrière firmly surrounding my erection, I drifted off in rapture and pure ecstasy. I was abruptly snatched back from my trip to Shangri-la when I felt her tugging at my hand that held her breast. She shouted, *"Jericho! Jericho! You can let go now! I am safe, Jericho!!"*

Her voice yanked me back into the present like a bucket of ice water. Struggling to regain my composure was like I was awakened suddenly from a wonderful dream. *"I-I-I was ar-ar-ar only trying to make sure you didn't fall."* My response sounded more like an excuse rather than a rescue.

Adjusting her top and bra straps, she said suspiciously, *"Well, you certainly did that alright. This trail requires such a hand from you in the leading. Maybe, if I led, you wouldn't have to work so hard."*

Still recovering, while trying to hide my embarrassment, I responded, *"Sure, I'll point the way from the rear,"* came out before I knew it.

The trail flattened out for a short distance, then entered its last upward swing through a steep gorge. Going almost straight up, put me directly behind those red pants rotating and bouncing around just in front of my face. Spread out, bent over, and struggling to get up the slope, her perspiration ran down her back and into the seat of those red pants. I would've loved to follow that trail straight into that heavenly place dominating my view.

As she slid back towards me a couple of times, I placed my hands on her butt to stop her sliding and balanced her. Touching her soft derrière as it nestled in my hands elevated my passion each time. Nearing the top, she lost her footing. Bent over, slipping and sliding, she came back down the hill towards me. I reached up and caught her butt in both hands. The impact of her large rear against my hands pushed my thumbs between her legs. Touching her heavenly moist softness as the spandex flexed inward with the force of her butt against my thumbs, pushing them into her soft insides. My thumbs penetrated that soft, moist heavenly place. Off balance, she tried to straighten up, as she groaned while trying to look back over her shoulder after her startle sound. Her full weight fell back against me with an even greater force. It carried us backward as I clutched her in my arms. Breaking her fall, we rolled downhill, locked together. Tumbling to the bottom, I ended up on top of her this time.

Lying between her legs, looking down into her beautiful eyes as she looked up into mine, she said, "What big eyes you have.

"Better to see you with, my dear." I responded.

She must have felt the stiffening of my resolve against

her pelvis because she jumped slightly and tried to slide from beneath me but couldn't

"Well, are you going to get up or build a home here?" She asked, with a strange expression on her face.

"Which do you prefer?" I retorted.

Without answering, she rolled me over and lay on top of me. Our eyes found each other again as I lay smiling.

"What big teeth you have." Before I could respond with the 'Better to eat you with my dear' retort, she continued. "You're not the kind of wolf that would take advantage of a helpless woman without a memory in the forest, are you?"

"Not if she hasn't ever known how incredible it is to make mad-passionate love on the forest floor."

Rolling away and getting to her feet, she looked down at me with an outstretched hand and said, "I guess I've never known such a wonderful pleasure."

She pulled me up, and our bodies came together again. She held me tightly against her body. Momentarily she pressed against me and then stepped away without looking at me. Turning away, then back towards me again, she took a step with her arms almost extended but caught herself. Placing one hand on her forehead and holding the other extended in my direction with the palm outward in a confused gesture, she blurted, *"Hold everything! Wait a minute! With all your help; pushing my rear up these hills, my ass probably has your handprints tattooed or branded on it. A stag, my ass. I'm the one who needs the gun, Mr. Moose. I don't think I would have needed your hands so much had we taken the road. What do you think, Bullwinkle?"*

Having thoroughly enjoyed every touch, rub, press, and roll with her, *"Whatever, Natasha,"* was my only reply.

I took the lead again, and we made it to the top of the plateau without mishap. When we resumed the hunt for clues to her identity, she seemed to have lost interest in it. Now, her face reflected a distracted gaze, constantly looking at me and then quickly away when I looked at her. Unlike on the trail, when she held onto my arm, now she maintained a few feet distance. It was as though she thought if we got too close, sparks might fly.

"Does anything around here seem familiar? Does it feel like you've been here before?" I ask, trying to get things back to the center.

"No. You said we wouldn't find anything here, and we haven't," she snapped.

"Yeah, I know, but we couldn't discount the possibility something might trigger a

response."

"Something triggered a response alright, but it had nothing to do with remembering who I am."

"What do you mean? Did I miss something?"

"No, I don't think you missed anything. If you ask me, you were all over everything that could be covered, and in that regard, I believe you touched it all."

"That's probably true, but I still feel like we may have missed something."

"Not as far as I could tell."

There seemed to be two different conversations going on, like we weren't talking about the same thing.

Working overtime trying to slice through all the confusion, I considered that some of her behavior may have seemed sensuous, flirtatious, or erotic to me, but now it seemed more likely my responses were to some of her characters, not her real personality. They seemed to pop out to fill the response void created when her real personality disappeared. Their appearance may depend on the response required. Having read a lot, some may even be vicarious inventions on her part, something like playing charade alone.

With her memory block in place, this girl's new world existed only in her head, which was populated by characters she locked behind unmarked doors to keep them hidden, maybe even from herself. Losing her memory unlocked the doors, but her mind's defense mechanism kept them from all running free at the same time. The lack of background information to explain what was happening and why her body may be reacting as if she is under a new kind of stress. Her mind may not have an inventory or a character capable of understanding what was happening to her now. Her entire assortment of characters may have never performed in the role or situation she now found herself in. Walking back around the road, I was in full observation mode; she maintained a specific distance. Something had changed in an unspoken way. Today gave us something different to think about concerning each other. We'd never been so close without some stressful event on her part bringing us together. Our touching was always an effort by me to console her. Never was there a conscious expression of desire. Even though the thought was on my mind constantly, I never dared show it openly. Headed back to the cabin, she made no cheerful comments about the scenery or wildlife; our silence said it all.

Her feminine mystique wasn't a facade any longer; now, it was what she was all about. She behaved as though she had truly been aroused by the contact and sexual innuendos on the trail, and the lack of a proper response seemed to have frightened her. Watching her eyes flash back and forth, I wondered, could her body's memory be trying to take control of her confused mind? Was it sending signals to her brain, which was overworking it, trying to adjust?

If she was a vibrant, sexually active young woman before her amnesia, like most hip-hoppers, her body could be having flashbacks. All the stimulating input today could be causing a sensory overload, and her behavior may not match her mindset. Perhaps, her body wanted to respond normally and satisfy its erotic impulses, but her confused mind keep saying no.

Normally, young women in today's modern hip-hop world respond to sexual stimulation or urges by gratifying them. Sex is like a reflex action, certainly no cause for consternation. In the hip hop world, total strangers meet in bars, clubs, and parties, strike up conversations over drinks, and are in bed together by early morning. Although there may be some underlying hope a relationship may develop, the urge for sexual gratification is not dependent on anything more than the act itself.

Her reaction to sexual arousal seemed to produce inner turmoil; she fretted over the proper response as though fighting with herself. Her body and behavior seemed to reflect not only readiness but also a willingness to the point of making enticing sexual innuendos and gestures. Inhibited by mental taboos regarding sex, her responses seemed disconnected and not reflective of the hip hop world from which she came. Confused now, both mentally and physically, I fear some inappropriate behavior may foreshadow a sensory overload or breakdown. It may express itself through some involuntary response or act that doesn't fit the situation at the time.

After that first night, conversations between us came easily. Now, what to talk about requires thought. Almost dark, we could feel a chill as we walked up the drive toward the cabin. Expressing relief at how good it was to be back at the cabin, conversation found its way back between us.

Walking through the door, she said, *"A-ah-h-h!! My, it's great to be home. I mean back here."* She looked at me quickly, then away again.

I pretended not to notice her reaction, then agreed, *"You got that right."* I followed with, *"I'm going to put a few logs in the fireplace and start dinner. Are you hungry?"* I asked, although I knew the answer.

"Famished and dirty. I'm going to take a long shower."

I thought about suggesting the steam chamber, but after the walk through the woods and the start-up time, I decided to wait for another day. Quickly frying some Tilapia filets that were marinating, I sautéed some mixed vegetables, steamed some wild rice, and tossed a salad to round out my hastily prepared dinner. However, we needed a conversation to go along with a wonderful meal.

Thinking back to our first encounter, I'd always thought she would wake up and provide all the answers to my questions. There wasn't any reason to think beyond that. It was the same once we learned she didn't have a memory. The hope and the thought that she would snap out of it at any moment became my reality. Today, I realized something. I decided to raise it while we ate.

She came out of the bathroom with her head wrapped in a towel, wearing my terry cloth bathrobe. So natural and comfortable, her face glowed. I envisioned her playing the perfect housewife role.

"Ah-a-a-a! That felt so wonderful! I stood under the hot running water as long as I could stand it. It's like I have new skin. I know you noticed, and I hope you don't mind me taking your robe. Hanging there after I got out of the shower, I'd put it on before I thought about it."

"Oh no! I don't mind. I never wore it anyway. It gives you that at-home look." With that statement, she looked up quickly. I felt the need to clarify. *"You know, comfortable, I mean."* Still scrambling, I said, *"I'll fix our plates. Have a seat."*

She commented as she took her seat, *"It smells wonderful. Is this fish?"*

"Yes, it's Tilapia. Have you ever had it?"

"No. I don't think so, but I love all kinds of fish."

"I have a special lime and herb marinade and my special way of breading and sautéing it. How does it taste?"

"Hum-m-m-m! It's great! It has such a rich flavor. I've never known a man that cooked so well. Some

woman is going to be very happy and lucky to get you."

"Well, I don't know about that. Would you accept my application if I applied?"

"Hell yes! Certainly! I would. I'd accept it right now if I knew I had an opening. You know good cooks are hard to find. Even with amnesia, I know that."

We both laughed. I continued, *"I didn't always cook, but I had to teach myself. Once up here, I improve my skill level. Being up here made me realize how important it is to do many things I never thought of doing. Speaking of things I never thought of, I realized had we gotten separated today, except that we were the only ones in the woods, had I needed to call you, what would I've said? Hey, girl in the red pants or Miss Lady with no memory? We need a temporary name for you. Something I can call you when you're not right next to me. Just, until your memory returns, of course."*

Inscrutably, she responded, *"I don't know Jericho. What if I like this temporary moniker? I might not want to remember my old name. Then what?*

"Oh, don't be silly! We'll pick something simple."

"Look at it from my perspective. Everyone calls you Jericho. Nobody calls you Richard, and you love it. What if you came up with a name like 'Sweet Cakes' or 'Snookums?' Even though people would laugh and look at me funny, I know I'll be loving it."

"What? Oh come on, I would never pick anything like that."

No longer able to keep a straight face, she burst into laughter. Only then did I realize the joke was on me. It occurred to me she might have felt she was the brunt of a joke when I suggested taking the shortcut through the woods, rather than walking around the road. Although that wasn't my intention, it may have seemed that way to her. She may have seen this as her chance to get even. Sensing her delight at putting one over on me, I tried to be just as good a sport as she by laughing as hard as I could at her little turnabout.

More than funny, her clever manipulation of the situation revealed not only that her mind was quick, but it was deceptively witty also. This was further evidence that a defense mechanism may be holding her intellect hostage to prevent her from remembering anything that identified her. I thought.

After having a good laugh to go along with an excellent dinner, she agreed and settled on Kay for Kimberly's initial, temporarily. She sat on her bed as I cleared the table. The day ended on such a good note. I didn't have to do or say anything to lift her spirits. She found a way to do that herself; things were looking up.

Not having to think of anything witty or inspirational to say was refreshing. Turning to face Kay, I hoped it wouldn't be a struggle for her to smile, but surprisingly she was fast asleep. Looking at her while pulling the covers over her, I wondered: *What had brought this delightful but possibly deadly enigma into my life, and whether or not Jordan's pessimistic appraisal foreshadowed my doom? A fait accompli, I could never let her leave. The question was, did I have the heart to kill her if she tried?*

Made in United States
Orlando, FL
20 October 2023